MISERABLE
HOLIDAY
STORIES

MISERABLE HOLIDAY STORIES

**20 Festive Failures
THAT ARE WORSE THAN YOURS!**

ALEX BERNSTEIN

Racehorse Publishing

Several of the pieces included here previously appeared in print or online at NewPopLit, The Big Jewel, Litro, The Legendary, BluePrintReview, Corvus, Craniotomic, eFiction, Hobo Pancakes, Dysfunctional Family Story and One Minute Plays. Please rush right now to each of these sites and check out great works by much less depressing authors.

Racehorse Publishing books may be purchased in bulk at special discounts for sales promotion, corporate gifts, fund-raising, or educational purposes. Special editions can also be created to specifications. For details, contact the Special Sales Department, Skyhorse Publishing, 307 West 36th Street, 11th Floor, New York, NY 10018 or info@skyhorsepublishing.com.

Racehorse Publishing™ is a pending trademark of Skyhorse Publishing, Inc.®, a Delaware corporation.

Visit our website at www.skyhorsepublishing.com.

10 9 8 7 6 5 4 3 2 1

Library of Congress Cataloging-in-Publication Data is available on file.

Cover photography: Getty Images

Print ISBN: 978-1-63158-581-4
Ebook ISBN: 978-1-63158-582-1

Printed in the United States of America

For Dad

Contents

MISERABLE
HOLIDAY
STORIES

Blue Christmas

"S O, Y'GOT A WEEK TO PULL OFF YER SHOW AND YER plumb stuck without a headliner?"

"That's about the size of it, yes."

"Christmas Eve's a busy night, son. Usually do three, four shows Christmas Eve."

"Right. Right. Well, I don't want to waste any more of your time."

I'm sitting in a shitty, dilapidated booth with torn red leather seats at the *Wishing Well*, the last "nightclub" in town to allow smoking. The club's empty except for us, the bartender, and a few lingering musicians, but there's still a thick, black fog in the room.

King Cassidy smiles at me, bites down on his stogie.

"No waste, son. What time you start?"

"Eight."

"Who's the opener?"

"I—we have jugglers. Two kids from the—from our Sunday school."

"Mmm," he says. "So, main show's at—"

"Nine."

"Mmm," he mutters again.

And three hundred pounds of bulging white jump suit, sunglasses, and an oily pompadour pulls out a tiny pocket calendar soaked in sweat. And with a swift motion, the King of Rock 'n Roll unholsters a pen from a zippered pocket on his left shoulder.

"Now, let's see . . ."

"Mr. Cassidy," I interrupt. "Obviously you've got some—talent. Why would you possibly want to do this?"

" 'Fraid I don't follow."

"I'm—I'm sorry. Could you just—could you just *stop* for a minute and be a—a regular person? It's just—it's difficult to talk to you this way."

The bartender and a couple of Cassidy's bandmates glance over at us. I forget I'm on his turf here, not mine. He looks at me—hurt? Angry? Hard to read Elvis.

"I'm sorry," I say. "I don't mean to waste your time. I just don't understand—"

"Ah do this for a living, son," he says.

"Yes, but not for *Jews*," I say.

He takes a long, deep breath, says nothing.

"I'm sorry," I say. "I'm sorry. This was my mistake."

The wind in the parking lot's torrential, about sixty miles an hour. I get in the car, turn the motor over, pray it won't stall in this crappy neighborhood. There's a rapping at my window—Cassidy. He's pissed. Got a gun or a crowbar or—he gestures for me to roll down the window. I roll it down. He shoves a manila folder at me, his black hair flapping in the wind.

"Take a look," he says.

I open the folder. It's his head shot. A huge, ultra-bright, smirking hound dog. Signed. An autograph?

"Other side," he says.

His résumé: acting, recordings, TV and stage appearances, his real name, phone, address. Real name?

I look at him, incredulous. He braces, holding his pomp for dear life.

"You're Jewish?"

He throws a DVD into the car, backs away.

"Need confirmation tomorrow, if we're a go," he says.

"Got it," I say and wave the résumé.

Julie and I sit in the living room, eating popcorn, staring at the television, mesmerized. On the infant monitor, Eddie snores quietly in his room. On TV, King Cassidy finishes a set, bellowing to an enraptured hall of Kiwanis.

"He's good," says Julie.

"I dunno," I say. "Maybe we could pull it off."

"Absolutely," says Julie. "Look at him. Can you believe you were going to spend money on Mort Sahl? This is a jackpot, Rob. He's perfect."

"He's just not perfect for the JCC. I mean, nobody's gonna come if I tell them it's Elvis."

"So, tell them it's Jewish Elvis."

I stare at her.

"Get him to sing *Blue Chanukah* or something. It's so obvious, Rob."

I feel a minor onset of hives suddenly creeping up the back of my neck.

"What if he doesn't go for it?"

"He's an Elvis impersonator! He's gotta have a sense of humor! Ask him."

"No?"

"No."

"Seriously? You mean—"

"Absolutely not," says a pissed-off Presley.

"Whoa! Wait! You wanted to do this—"

"This isn't a game to me, Mr. Chaykin—"

"Rob—"

"I take my profession very serious."

"*You're Jewish and you're Elvis!* Come on! There's gotta be other Jewish Elvises out there!"

"Well, call them, then. 'Cause I'll be no party to mockery."

"Cassidy . . . look . . . it's just . . . I'm afraid that people . . . members of this community won't show up for an Elvis concert. It's not that your show isn't good. It's just that this is an extremely conservative group and *Viva Las Vegas* isn't something they usually associate with."

"Not my problem," he sighs.

"I know. I just—I want to get an audience for you. I want the show to be good."

"Mr. Chaykin, you bring your crowd in—with no billing as *Jewish Elvis*—and I'll give 'em a show they'll remember. *Guaranteed.*"

I hear his deep, mammoth cave-breathing waiting for me. God, I've got less than a week.

"Okay," I say. "Okay. I'll get them in."

Work.

Everything is Christmas, Christmas, Christmas. Yeah, okay, they've got a tiny electric menorah, some decorations. An eighth of the staff's Jewish after all. But really, it's all Christmas. There's an incredible tree. The office is littered with cookies, cards, poinsettias. People have started wearing snowman pins and Christmas tree ties, collecting toys for the underprivileged. Everyone's talking about shopping, family, holiday vacations, and the massive, upcoming office Christmas party. Carols permeate the ether.

Bobby Bloom leans into my cubicle.

"Tell me you didn't get King Cassidy for your party?"

"Yup. Yup. I did."

"Score!"

Bobby daps me, calls over to the adjacent cubes.

"You literally forget this guy isn't the real thing," he says. "That's how good he is!"

"Really?" says Peggy Newley, eyes lit up, leaning back from her desk. "Is he young Elvis—or—"

"Late Elvis," says Bobby. "Almost near-death Elvis. He must weigh—what—350 pounds?"

"250 to 275," I say.

"He's slimmed down. But man, he could belt!"

"He's great," I agree.

Joey Roemer leans in.

"I saw King Cassidy at my old company's party last year. Unbelievable."

"We should get him for our party!" says Peggy.

"I dunno," I say. "He's got a pretty tight schedule."

They return to their cubes. I breathe. Back to work, work. Peggy peeks over my cube, whispers.

"Rob—could I get a ticket to your show?"

"Uhm—well—it's—it's—"

"Jews only?"

"No! It's—it's invitation only. Y'know?"

She smiles, politely.

"Okay," she says, disappointed. "Thought you needed the money."

Julie sorts through mail in the kitchen. In the living room, Eddie wobbles to Elvis's rendition of *Here comes*

Santa Claus, here comes Santa Claus, right down Santa Claus Lane while staring at soundless *Backyardigans* on TV. *God, what's she thinking?*

"You had to do that? It's not bad enough as it is?"

"He loves it," she says. "Look at him."

I turn off the music. Eddie looks at me, sad, confused. I kiss him and turn up the cartoon.

"Hey, Sport. How are you?"

"Here comes Santa Claus! Here comes Santa Claus!"

"Well . . . he's not coming here, bud."

"Why not?"

"Because we don't do that."

"Why not?"

"Because we just don't, Eddie. We did Chanukah last week. Remember how great that was? We even left up the lights, the menorah—"

He stares at me, as if I've ripped his most blessed *Ugly Doll* away, which I guess I have.

"I want to do Christmas."

"I know you do, honey. But we don't—"

The lips tremble. Here we go.

"Hey! Hey! Look what I found!" I pull a DVD out of my briefcase. "Dinosaurs! A movie about dinosaurs!"

"They celebrate Christmas?"

"No—they—they just eat things and fight and chase each other. And in this one they end up in New York! It's got outtakes and—"

He stares at it, deciding.

"Look, Mom!" he says. "Dinosaurs!"

"Very cool, honey. Why don't you put it on?"

He puts it in the DVD player, settles into his bean bag chair. I go back to the kitchen.

"You're uptight," she says.

"Yeah? And you're not helping."

"Please. Half his class is Jewish. They talk Chanukah all month long."

"If he went to *Yavneh* he'd never even hear about Christmas!"

"If we locked him in the closet he wouldn't either. Why don't we do that?"

"You don't have to make it more difficult."

"By buying a record?"

"It's cruel, Julie."

"Cruel?"

"It's bad enough he has to hear about it all day long— then you stick it in his face!"

Here comes Santa Claus, here comes—

"Don't touch the CD player, Eddie!"

Julie stares at me, fuming.

"See?" I say. "He doesn't need to be more confused than he already is."

"You hired Elvis!"

"It was that or cancel! I do everything I can to keep the community center together by myself! It would be nice if I could have a little more—"

The house phone rings. I pick it up.

"Dr. Berman? Yes, I spoke to him. He'll work out fine. Yes, I know. No Christmas songs. I've seen him, sir. There's plenty of other material he can do. No need to be uncomfortable. He's very talented. Yes, I believe he'll take requests if they're within his repertoire. Yes. I'll get the contract signed tomorrow. Good night."

I look over and see Julie's ferreted Cassidy's contract out of my brief. And she's flipping through the pages, mouth agape.

"Julie—"

"A hundred dollars?"

"Julie—"

"You've got eight hundred people coming!"

"No—no—six-fifty—maybe seven hundred, tops."

"Rob!"

"You know what the center lost this year? You know what it costs just to light that room for one night?! This barely covers expenses!"

She digs through the junk drawer, pulls out our check-book, writes.

"What are you—"

She rips out a check, hands it to me. $500.

"You're kidding me."

"We can afford it. Everyone coming to this show can afford it."

"That's not the point."

"You give him this check, Rob."

"No."

"You give it to him, or *I'll* give it to him. I don't care which."

"Jesus, Julie!"

"*Jesus!*" says Eddie, watching dinosaurs.

"He's doing you a favor!" she says. "You won't even let him sing Christmas songs!"

"It's my money!" I yell. "My money!"

"You give him the check or stay at work on Christmas," she says and walks out of the room.

And in the living room, Eddie looks at me, hopeful.

"When are we getting the tree?"

Jelvis. Melvis. Schmelvis.

Surfing the net. 1:30 in the morning.

Elvis Prestein. Rebbe Elvis. Kosher Elvis.

I'm pissed at Julie. Pissed at the JCC, at the JCC Board of Directors, at Dr. Berman for approving Cassidy in the first place and then hamstringing me to run the thing. *I'm just the goddamn Treasurer, for Christ sake!* I'm pissed at everyone, everything, everywhere. Jews everywhere.

Klez Elvis.

I'll expense the $500. Charge it back to them. Somehow, I'll get my money back. But—I keep telling myself—that's not the point. This shouldn't even be happening. I should've just canceled.

Surfing, I see a virtual pageant of all Jewish Elvises the world has to offer. Elvis jumpsuits with *tallit*, blue, white and gold lamé, huge Star of David gold chains. They sing Elvis tunes reworked with Jewish and Yiddish phrases. All are one-joke wonders. Embarrassing. Truly, utterly awful. And all are four times as expensive as Cassidy.

And what's wrong with liking Christmas? Everyone likes Christmas. It's not just a Christian holiday. Okay, the whole birth of Christ thing is Christian but not—not what we Americans and society have turned the holiday into. And even if it is ultimately a birth-of-Christ thing—

well, so what? I can't appreciate the music? The decorations? *Miracle on 34th Street?*

Hey, *I* wanted a Christmas tree when I was four years old. And five. And six. And seventeen. Eighteen. Thirty-eight. Why shouldn't Eddie? So, he should get screwed because I got screwed?

Cassidy's house is normal. Smaller than mine and in a B-minus neighborhood. But nice. Not the trailer park I'd expect of a celebrity impersonator. He certainly has better Chanukah lights than I do, I'll give him that. Inside it's simple. Nice. Old world. Steam heat from radiators. Dull, tan, run-down wallpaper. His two kids are normal. Cute even. Blue and white lights decorate his den and he still has a few menorahs out. And no Chanukah bush.

There are a couple pictures of the real Elvis, some framed concert tickets, a gold record—hardly the memorabilia you'd expect. Almost disappointing, really.

"There are some conditions here," I say, as he glances through the contract. "You can't perform any Christmas songs. No Christmas, no Christ, no Santa Claus. No—no—I don't know—gospel?"

He stares at me, bored.

"I'm sorry," I say. "I have to make this speech. If it were up to me—you could perform whatever you like. But it's not. I don't know if this will limit your act—"

Cassidy signs, hands me the contract.

"Guess that'll do it," he says.

"Great. Thanks," I say, then jokingly, "Not much of a shrine."

"More in storage," he says.

We head to the door. I finger the envelope in my pocket. The check. My hand grips it like a vise. I can let go. I can. I can.

"Well . . ." I say, "you realize what a tight budget we're on. Building the new community center. Everybody donating their time. I don't take a penny, myself. It's all volunteer."

He hands me my coat.

"I just don't want you to think we don't—appreci-ate—what you're doing. Because—because—"

"Mr. Chaykin," he says. "I been trying to play yer cen-ter for ten years now. Every year I offer and every year y'turn me down. Who cancelled?"

"Mort Sahl."

He nods, unsurprised.

"Family thing?"

"Kidney operation."

He opens the door. The wind outside is bitter.

"I tell you my father was Cantor at Adath Israel when I was in grade school?"

"No," I say.

"Mm. I went to Yavneh first through third grade."

"Really?"

"Yep. Hated it. Hated the kids. Hated the temple. Thought it was unbelievably boring. Only memory I have of Yavneh—one day during recess, half the boys held me down on the slide and rolled an old tire over me. Big laughs. After my father died, I said screw it. Didn't go to temple, church. Didn't do nothin'."

From the kitchen, a tired dishwasher chugs to life.

"But having my own kids, I understand what my father did. He sang. Beautiful bright tenor. Singing was everything. He connected on his own terms."

He looks toward the street.

"Not about money for me," he says.

And I stand alone outside his doorway, feeling the cold night air at my neck. So, it doesn't matter. He doesn't care about money. I'm off the hook. So easy to walk away. But I leave the extra check in his mailbox.

Christmas Eve.

A packed auditorium. Every Jewish person in town is here tonight. Everyone's here because it's social—a good event, a good charity—and what else do these people have to do tonight? A well-placed weapon of destruction could take out the whole community in two seconds.

The jugglers—two kids in their late teens—close to a standing ovation.

"Thank you!" says a juggler. "King Cassidy will be up in just a minute!"

Some cheers. Some members of the crowd get up, coats in hand, and file toward the exit. My good community. Ten minutes later, the lights dim. A single white spotlight shines onstage. The back of a grossly overweight white jumpsuit begins to disenvelope from a kneeling huddle. A husky, breathy baritone begins to sing, a cappella.

A-don o-lam

Julie's hand grips mine. The crowd—the crowd is—transfixed?

Asher ma-Ia

Cassidy turns toward us, in full regalia, issuing a focused, ethereal sound . . .

B'terem kol y'tzer nivrah

I realize everyone—myself included—is singing with him.

B-yet-hasa v-he-esa kol, a-za-ay melech sh'monekrah. A-don olam

He finishes. The audience applauds, cheers, thrilled. Julie—a lot of people, actually—are *crying*. Cassidy grins, struts across the stage.

"Thank y'very much," he says. "Mah momma named me KC. But you kin call me Cassidy. Y'all ready for some fun?"

The crowd cheers.

"Well, then, let's get it on."

An orchestra of canned music bursts to life, and Cassidy begins to twitch.

That's alright now, mama. That's alright with you. That's alright now, mama, just anyway you do. That's alright.

Cassidy blows through *Jailhouse Rock, Don't Be Cruel, Puppet on a String, Trouble, I Want You I Need You I Love You, Return to Sender, Teddy Bear, Don't, All Shook Up, Suspicious Minds, Stuck on You, Can't Help Falling in Love, Burning Love, Bigger Hunk of Love, Love Me Tender, Blue Suede Shoes, Are You Lonesome Tonight, Eleanor Rigby* and *Hound Dog.* And before you know it, the evening's half over. He sings

Dreidel, Dreidel, Dreidel and actually stops the show for a candlelit prayer of *Ma'oz-Tzur.*

He sings *Blue Chanukah,* winking and smiling at Julie and all the women in the audience. They laugh. They love it. *Such a bubby!*

After two hours and two encores of rambling and rocking, Cassidy, drenched in sweat, slows things to a halt and speaks, in confession, to the audience.

"My, my, my," he says. "Thank y'all so much for coming together on this cold, frosty night. My final song, ladies and gentlemen, was written by a man named Israel Baline, a Jewish man who became America's greatest modern-day composer. And no matter what words he wrote, his music spoke of a deeper understanding of faith—a faith that came right straight from the center of his heart."

And Cassidy turns to me.

Uh oh.

"I'd like to dedicate this song to Robert Chaykin, who helped make my dream of being with you tonight, a reality."

People look at me, some sniggering, some wary, confused. I can feel the hives creeping across my back. In a steady, quiet voice, KC begins.

And suddenly the entire crowd listens to the perfect, rising melody of a *White Christmas*—just like the one they used to know. And the ether rises with images of glistening treetops and those playful children hearing sleigh bells in the snow.

And I'm frozen. *Oh my God. He did it! He screwed me! He couldn't let it go! How could he do this? Bastard!* I imagine congregants setting fire to the building, the roof caving in, rocks thrown at my house. And I'm flush red—but—but—I realize—everyone's quiet, listening. And a few seats over I hear in a whisper . . .

Irving Berlin was Jewish?

Eddie tugs on my arm. His head bobs and he smiles at me, so happy. Julie smiles and sings in her atonal warble. *Everyone* is singing, in one shining, brilliant voice. *How do they all know this song?* Do all Jews have Christmas albums?

"Rob Chaykin, ladies and gentlemen," says Cassidy.

And everyone claps for me. For me? Dumbly, I wave, smile.

"Have a good night and a very happy holiday season," he says.

And King Cassidy leaves the building.

Julie cradles sleepy Eddie on her shoulder, her coat wrapped around him. She takes my arm and we shuffle out with the rest of the crowd. Christmas is over. Chanukah's over.

Maybe next year we'll get a tree.

Coloring Books

A SMALL BOOKSTORE AT THE MALL, ALL DECKED OUT FOR the holiday shopping season. Tinsel, greenery, and baubles adorn the bookshelves. MICHAEL, a young, fragile child approaches the front desk and speaks to the energetic CLERK, who wears an apron and has candy canes hanging from his glasses. Michael holds up a gift certificate.

MICHAEL: I received this gift certificate for Chanukah and I'd like to spend it.

CLERK: Well, that's terrific. What are you interested in?

MICHAEL: Do you have coloring books?

CLERK: Are you kidding? We're the biggest bookstore in the tri-state! We've got tons of coloring books!

MICHAEL: Oh great.

Clerk pulls out a mammoth, colorful volume and shows it to Michael.

CLERK: Here's one that just came in. It's the latest in the *Guggenheim Fractal Art* series! Featuring chaotic illustrations of crystal growth and fluid turbulence!

Michael looks through the book and recoils, queasy.

MICHAEL: I don't think I like those. They're kind of making me sick.

Clerk puts that book away and brings out another with large, ornate prints in it.

CLERK: No problem! Say—we just got in this delightful new series on the intricacies of Elizabethan architecture. The detail is microscopic!

Michael flips through and is perplexed.

MICHAEL: This looks strange and complicated.

Michael hands it back. Clerk puts it away.

CLERK: Are you more into fashion coloring?

MICHAEL: No.

Clerk brings out a book with actual linens dangling from the edges.

CLERK: Because we just got in *Flapper Designs of the Roaring 20s*. And! It comes with an old-fashioned eighteen-page *Bartender's Almanac*.

MICHAEL: I don't know what that is. But I don't like it.

Clerk puts the design book away and brings out what appears to be a thick, dirty phone book.

CLERK: Say! What you might like then, is our *Mindfulness Meditation* series. Over four thousand pages of deeply repetitive ocean imagery. You can't *not* be tranquil when you color these! *Ommmmmmm!*

Michael looks away, frightened.

MICHAEL: Do you—do you have any—

CLERK: Yes?

MICHAEL: Do you have any with—with *SpongeBob*?

CLERK: The cartoon?

MICHAEL: Yes.

CLERK: You're a troublemaker, aren't you?

MICHAEL: What?

CLERK: Of course, we don't have *SpongeBob*! We sell the world's finest coloring books! Guides to help you achieve one-ness and enlightenment and bliss!

Michael withdraws a small box and holds it up.

MICHAEL: But—I got these crayons–and I want to color.

CLERK: Well—I'm sorry but . . . *wait!*

Clerk pulls out a flimsy, flat pamphlet.

CLERK: Yes! I do have this one book on aquatic bottom-feeders! I believe there's a–*yes!* Yes! HA! There it is! *There's your sponge right there on page eight!*

Michael looks through the book and perks up. He hands the Clerk the gift certificate.

MICHAEL: Okay, I'll take it.

CLERK: Terrific. Now . . . I'll need to see some ID.

MICHAEL: Why?

CLERK: It's the law. You've got to be eighteen to buy a coloring book.

Driving Lesson

ONE BRIGHT WINTER MORNING, SHORTLY BEFORE Christmas, my dad decided to teach me how to drive on the highway in the middle of a blizzard. We were approaching I-75—one of the two major expressways in Cincinnati—and at that point I'd never merged onto a highway in *any* weather, much less a blizzard. So, I was in no way what you'd call prepared. I was nervous as I tried to merge, and I turned the steering wheel a hair too hard to the left. Suddenly, the car skidded and spun 180 degrees and was now driving toward oncoming traffic.

Whether it was the surreal, heavy snowfall, or a clouded lens of pure fear, the traffic—trucks, cars, everything—came at us like a glittering, slow motion stampede.

My father yelled, "*Get out of the car!*"

I shoved open my door and jumped into a hunkered walking position—and watched as the car continued to slowly slide forward at about five miles per hour. Dad, also now out of the car, yelled to me.

"Did you put it in park?"

I stared at him. *Did I what?*

Beautiful, life-threatening vehicles skated past us, caroming off the side rail, slipping into ditches. And it occurred to me how typical this was of me and my dad. Being thrust into some insane, completely preventable pitfall of our own creation.

Together, we stood in deep, tread-marked ice, watching his poor Chevy Caprice slide unerringly toward an immense eighteen-wheeler, like some automated David taking on a chrome Goliath.

We were extremely lucky. No one got hurt. No one pressed charges. And despite barreling headlong into the grill of the truck, our Caprice suffered only a crushed headlight. The eighteen-wheeler, of course, remained in perfect condition.

The 22

SATURDAY, DECEMBER 23. MOTEL 6—ROOM 143. Seventy-two degrees.

Jim Chase, fifty-eight, lanky with blond crew cut, sits wrapped in a towel on his bed, talking on the room phone. The towel has holes in it. The air conditioner is loud and on high. Jim's face is flushed, and he coughs incessantly.

"I just want some fresh towels sent up!" Jim says into the phone. "This is the third time I've called. How fucking difficult is it to just get some goddamn towels?! Thank you."

Jim hangs up. Peripherally, a blue jay lands outside his motel room window. But Jim doesn't see the blue jay, because Jim has no peripheral vision; which is to say that if you came at him straight on, he'd see you fine, but if you approached him from the side, he wouldn't even register you as existing. From the side, you would be the perfect, invisible ninja.

Jim grabs his obsolete 2010 Motorola cell phone and hits redial.

"Hi. It's Jim again. I'm having car trouble. My goddamn rental actually seized on me this morning. Can you believe that? Yeah, they're working on it, but I'm running about an hour late. No, they said they can't get a replacement for three hours because of the holidays. But I'll take a cab. No big—no—no, don't do that—don't do that—I can—you're sure? Really? It's no—"

Jim opens his laptop and hits the "on" button. Immediately: BEEP BEEP BEEP BEEP BEEP BEEP BEEP BEEP

"Oh—oh Jesus—Jesus! I just got this thing fixed two days ago. It's my goddamn laptop—I've got a blue screen. This is not my goddamn morning!"

Jim hits the "on" button several times. Nothing happens. He opens and closes the cover. The beeping continues.

"Fuck," he mumbles. "Fuck, fuck. Hold on—"

He shoves the laptop under a pillow. The beeping continues, muffled.

"Okay, fixed," says Jim. "Look, I'll take a cab. I—uh-huh? You sure you don't mind? Okay—alright—there's a—"

He looks out the window.

"There's a—a Jolly Trolley across the street. Next to—Electronic Liquidators—yeah, on the 22. You know where it is? Great. You're sure? It's no big—no, that's a big help. Thank you. Great. Thank you. See you."

BEEP BEEP BEEP BEEP BEEP BEEP BEEP

Kenilworth, New Jersey. 210 Naomi Ave. Dan Morgan, twenty-four, a cop, stands in the backyard of the Mohr residence. He holds Louis Mohr's Marlin 44 mag rifle and writes out a court summons. Earlier that morning, Louis Mohr, eighty-two, after reading his mail, went into his backyard and started firing the rifle into the shrubs against the back fence, putting bullet holes into his neighbor Jerry's garage. Louis got off twelve shots before the police arrived. Ten minutes after that Louis's daughter Kaye, forty-six, showed up.

"Danny," says Kaye, "I am so, so sorry. I promise you this will *never* happen again."

"No problem, Kaye."

"Why's he taking my Marlin?! Gimme my fuckin' Marlin!" says Louis.

"You get in the house and you *stay there*," says Kaye to Louis.

Inside the house. Kaye reads the letter from Wells Fargo. Louis, on the couch, watches a bass fishing show on TV.

"*Oh my god,*" says Kaye.

"Goddamn deer," mutters Louis.

"You haven't paid your mortgage in *21 months?!*"

"Why should I? Won't change anything! Won't clear 'em out! Goddamn deer."

"When were you gonna tell me about this?"

"Nothing to tell."

"I swear to god, Dad. What were you thinking? You're just gonna wait till the police come and lock you out?"

"*It's not my fault!* It's the goddamn—"

"This has *nothing* to do with deer, Dad. This has to do with you being fucking insane! Why the fuck do you do this to me?!"

"It's not my fault!"

"Who's your loan officer?"

"Who cares," he mumbles.

Kaye shuffles through the papers, finds a foreclosure notice.

"Here. Okay. Oh—hey, Dad—"

She shows Louis the note.

"*This* is your loan officer?"

"Maybe."

"Oh shit."

Jim Chase, in blue Oxford shirt and blue slacks, walks from the Motel 6 to the edge of Route 22 with his beeping laptop under his arm and waits for the rushing traffic to pause. A pause comes and Jim darts to the center guardrail, climbs over and waits for another break in traffic. After a moment, he dashes the rest of the way and enters Electronic Liquidators, home of the Nerd Specialists.

Seventy-three degrees.

Louis Mohr's house. Kaye, on the phone, paces. Louis, on the couch, watches men prepare a bass fishing lure on TV.

"I'm calling about loan number 400029546," says Kaye.

"I can help you," says a woman with a slight Southern lilt in her voice.

"Is this Randi Saenz?" asks Kaye.

"Yes, it is. Is this Mrs. Mohr?"

"This is—this is—Kaye Mohr. Louis Mohr's daughter."

There's a pause on the other end of the line.

"Kaye Mohr—of Bound Brook?"

"That's right."

"Kaye!?"

"Randi?"

"Kaye! Kaye! Oh my god! Oh my god! Kaye Mohr! Oh my god!"

"Hi, Randi. How are you?"

"How are you!?"

"Okay. Good. You know—I—"

"Are you still in Bound Brook? Kaye Mercer now, right?"

"No, no—just Kaye Mohr again."

"Oh—I saw you had that status change—when was it—June?"

"Yeah. It's been a long year. Randi—"

"God—what is it—thirty-five years? I *love* all the pictures you post!"

"Yeah. I really don't go on as much as I used to—"

"Oh, I live on there! Still! I was just on ten minutes ago! I love that talent night picture you posted with everyone in the back—and I've got that terrible scream—"

"Randi—I would love to catch up with you—but—could we just talk about my father's mortgage for a second?"

"Oh—oh—of course! Of course! Hold on—it's—right in front of me."

Louis shifts on the couch.

"Goddamn deer—" he says.

"Oh—*oh my*," says Randi. "You know he's gotten a final foreclosure notice?"

"Yes, I know. That's why I'm calling. Randi, honestly, I just saw this today for the first time, ever. See, my father—he suffers from certain mental deficiencies—"

"The hell I do!"

"Shh!" says Kaye, swatting him.

"We've made several attempts to contact him," says Randi.

"I know. I understand that, Randi," says Kaye. "But honestly, anything I can do to make this go away would be really, incredibly—"

"I wish I could help you, Kaye, but the paperwork's done. We're all set to—"

"Randi—I could bring you a check *right now*. Seriously. You'd be the hero of the bank, Randi. We could make this all go away. Think of that."

"Right now?"

"What's the balance? Twenty-one months? So, it's what—"

"Twenty-nine thousand, three hundred and forty-three dollars."

Kaye takes a deep breath, swallows. She girds herself.

"Yes—that's fine," says Kaye. She covers up the phone and sneers in Louis's ear. *"It's just every last cent I have in the goddamn world!"* She returns to the phone. "That's perfect. Randi. Twenty-nine, three forty-three. I can bring the whole thing in."

"Well, I do have an appointment—"

"I'll be there in one minute, Randi. We can wrap this whole thing up!"

"Oh—well, oh sure. Come on over!"

"Great! Randi—you're a peach!"

"Oh," says Randi.

"What?" says Kaye.

"Oh—look at that."

"What?"

"I just flipped over to FB for one second—"

"Randi—"

"And you're not there."

"Randi—"

"Did you—did you de-friend me, Kaye?"

"I—"

"You did. You de-friended me."

"Randi—Randi—I don't—I don't do Facebook at all anymore—honestly—it's been such a long—"

"You posted a comment to Jill Krementz this morning. And there you are commenting on Bobby Meisner's bowling party picture. Huh."

"Randi—please—I can be there in ten minutes. Maybe we can go get a bite to eat? Talk about talent night. Please. For my dad's sake—"

"*Tick-ridden bastards,*" says Louis.

"Just let me clear this little thing up, Randi. Okay? Let me make everything good again. Please?"

Kaye waits.

"Oh. Sure. Sure. Of course," says Randi. "Come in. Come in. We'll clear the whole thing right up."

"Thank you! Thank you so much, Randi. I can't tell you how much I appreciate this."

"No problem."

Kaye hangs up. She turns to Louis.

"*Stay here and don't move!*" says Kaye, and she rushes out.

Louis grumbles, watches men fish on TV. The day's mail on the stained coffee table stares at him, belligerent, makes him anxious, angry. And then he sees it. There, among the letters, that thing—that—*that deer—the deer itself!*—towering, wistful, doe-eyed, proud, challenging, *boastful!* That goddamn, goddamn—and—*25 percent off, this weekend only!*

Jesus, nineteen, short and portly with thick sideburns and a nickel-sized stud in his earlobe, taps a reset button on Jim's laptop. The beeping stops. He flips the laptop over and gives a bored look.

"She dead. Gotta get a new one."

"Dead? I just got it fixed last week."

Jesus shrugs.

"Dead."

"Aren't you going to do a diagnostic?"

"Just did. She dead."

"You just flipped it over."

Jesus shrugs.

"I want a diagnostic. A full diagnostic," says Jim.

"I know this model. Piece a shit. I know when she dead. And she dead."

"You didn't do a full diagnostic!" Jim points to a nearby poster of a friendly, eager Caucasian Nerd Specialist holding up a sign for a WORLD-CLASS, 12-POINT DIAGNOSTIC.

"Don't need it."

"I want to talk to a manager."

"I'm the manager."

Jim coughs incessantly. He stares, coldly, at Jesus. Jesus shifts, bored.

"I just fixed this goddamn thing last week!" says Jim. "I put in a new SSD drive—whatever the fuck that is—for $400!"

"Should've bought new one."

"*Jesus Christ!*" says Jim. "*What the hell kind of nerd are you?!* You don't even *look* like a nerd! Listen—I use Nerd Specialists in Albany—and *those are quality nerds!* If you think this is quality nerd service—your idea of nerd service is *way* under par!"

"Mm," says Jesus.

Peripherally, a growing line of customers grunt and shift. But Jim sees none of them because he has no peripheral vision.

"I'll tell you what I want. I want *that* service!" Jim says pointing to the cheerful poster. "I want the goddamn, 12-step, world-class diagnostic *everything! Full-on Nerd Service!*"

Jesus shrugs, sticks a sheet in front of Jim.

"Name, address, credit card, driver's license," he says, handing Jim a pen.

"*Whatever!*" sneers Jim and he starts writing.

In the back room of Nerd Specialists—a place commercially trademarked "The Nerd Cave"—Toi, a seventeen-year-old with a McCartney haircut and enough eyebrow rings to hold a shower curtain, watches Jesus's hands dance across a keyboard.

"S'up?" says Toi.

"'Nother asshole," says Jesus.

"Give you his driver's license?"

"Yup."

"Assholes never learn," says Toi.

Kaye Mohr stands outside the Westfield Wells Fargo branch, holding a small white envelope. She peers inside, tapping on the glass door with a key. Inside, the bank is dark. She taps louder and louder, accidentally nicking the glass.

The Jolly Trolley.

Jim Chase sits at a table with an outstanding view of the 22 and his Motel 6 across the street. He holds up a spoon and stares at his upside-down reflection. He coughs. His untouched beer gets warmer.

Seventy-four degrees.

A large-boned, platinum blonde with a hefty set of worn, rubber band–bound folders stands over him.

"Jim Chase?" she says.

"Randi?" he says. He stands and shakes her hand. "Thanks for coming all the way out here!"

"No problem!"

She sits.

"Listen," he says. "Al says you've taken over great for him—haven't missed a beat. How's he liking retirement?"

"A little too much! Never off the links!"

"Why should he—with this weather?! Jesus! Is it always this hot in December?!"

"No—no—it's a fluke—"

"Can I get you something to drink?" says a mysterious waitress.

"Well, I guess we're being casual?" says Randi, grinning and eyeing Jim's beer.

"Hell, it's Saturday!" says Jim.

"Can you do a Mojito?" says Randi.

Fifteen minutes later. Randi pokes through the bottom of a Cobb salad. Her cell phone rings. She ignores it. Near Jim sit the remains of a blood-red steak and a third beer. He pores through folders, property lists.

"Uh-huh, uh-huh . . . and this one's—"

"East Brunswick. That's the four bedroom, three-and-a-half bath. They cleared out a week ago."

"Guy with the chainsaw?"

"It's not as bad as everyone says. Two walls in the kitchen, a chandelier—thing, some drywall. We'll have it spick-and-span in a week."

"Uh-huh," Jim makes a notation on a ratty, dog-eared map. "These two are near each other, right? We can hit 'em together—"

The waitress returns with Jim's Visa card.

"I'm sorry, sir," she says. "Your card was declined. Do you have another?"

Randi's cell phone rings. She ignores it.

Wells Fargo. Kaye leans up against the glass door, annoyed, sweating, fanning herself. She calls on her cell phone. No answer.

The Jolly Trolley.

The waitress returns Randi's Visa card to her.

"I told you those aren't my goddamn charges!" says Jim into his cell phone. "I was never in Texas! No—I need you to clear it off, now. *Now!* I can't wait three days! Lemme speak to your supervisor! *You're* the supervisor? *Christ!*"

"Jim—" says Randi.

"Let me talk to your—your—"

"Jim, hang up. Hang up. It's okay."

He looks at her. She nods.

"It's okay. I took care of it."

"I—my card's blocked for three goddamn—"

"I know."

"Where's the—"

"I took care of it. No big deal."

"You expense that!" he says, coughing incessantly.

"I will," she says.

Jim hangs up, looks out the window, and returns to the property lists.

"Kenilworth? Mohr?"

"Couldn't work it out."

Jim reads the notes.

"Completely unresponsive . . . ?" asks Jim. "He got all the notices?"

"I have certified receipts. It was twenty-one months."

"Yeah. Mm. Veteran. You really couldn't work it out?" He looks out the window.

"I did everything I could," sighs Randi.

She sets an official document before him. He signs.

"And the sheriff'll be there——?"

"Tuesday."

Lord & Taylor.

Kaye Mohr drowns herself in shoes. She won't buy anything. She'll just look. Maybe try on a—oh hell, *why shouldn't she buy anything!?* Why shouldn't she baby herself!? It's the frigging holidays! It's not like she's in Manhattan spending $400 on some boutique brand! And red red red red red red red red red red red red red looks so good on her perfect, little—

"*Kaye!*" says Jody Peerless, peering out from a nearby pile of shoes.

"I *love* those!" says Jody. "Those are *so* you!"

Shit shit shit.

"You think?" asks Kaye.

"Absotively!" says Jody, holding up a pair of black pumps. "We're headed for the Caribbean tomorrow—and I need a pair of dress shoes."

Ten feet away, Mike and Jordan Peerless lean on each other, transfixed in boredom by cell phone games.

"Those are nice," says Kaye.

"Holiday plans?" says Jody.

"Just me and Dad."

"No Tommy?"

"He's with his father skiing."

"Y'know," says Jody, "I am *so* jealous. I wish I could trade places with you and do nothing! That would be Heaven!"

The Jolly Trolley.

Jim looks through property lists. Randi stares at him.

"Y'know, Jim," says Randi, "I don't think I've *ever* seen you on Facebook."

"Maplewood. Maplewood? Newark," says Jim, staring at regional foreclosure maps.

"Okay, I know—I know that's not a terribly professional thing to say, but we *are* being business casual! I know what you're thinking. It's a complete waste of time. But I'll tell you ... I've caught up with so many people I've known throughout my life—grade school, high school—and they're on there, posting all the time!"

"Camden? Six houses in Camden? God."

"It's like a little museum of everyone you've ever known—all under glass. Like—like eBay—but with people instead of junk. Y'know what, Jim?"

Jim reads through properties.

"I have—and I say this not to brag but just because it's true—today, *I have two thousand friends.* Isn't that terribly exciting?! Just this morning! *Two thousand!* Okay, that's it. I got it out of my system!"

Jim looks up, stares at her, blankly.

"I know what you're thinking! Those are like teenage numbers! I mean—I don't *know 'em*-know 'em. Y'know? Most are just online folks, friends of friends of friends— but still—it's like a little growing universe, all in one place!"

"Uh-huh."

"But I don't do TikTok or anything like that," says Randi. "That's just stupid."

"Okay," says Jim.

"So ... ?" says Randi, leaning excitedly toward him.

"Uh," says Jim.

"How many? I mean, if it's not *too* intrusive—"

"What?" says Jim.

"Friends?" says Randi.

"Friends—?"

"How many do you have?"

Jim looks at her, strangely.

"I've never counted," says Jim.

Randi laughs a loud *yowl*.

"You don't have to count! The number's counted right there for you!"

Jim says nothing, fidgets, looks at the maps. Randi's eyes go wide.

"Oh my—oh my—*you're in single digits, aren't you? That's it, isn't it?"*

"Maybe if we stick to New Brunswick, and stay north of—"

"You know what I'll do? I'll tell you what—I'll send a friend suggestion to some of the folks up in Albany, and in REO—there are *so* many people—you probably know half of them—" Randi pulls out her iPhone. "This'll just take a second."

Jim watches her like a squirrel in a tree watching an approaching bulldozer.

"What's that?" says Jim.

"This? My iPhone?" says Randi. "So, what are you under? Chase? J. Chase? Jim Chase? You use another name? Do you have a picture?"

"Uh," says Jim.

"Show me," says Randi. She takes Jim's hand, and presses the phone firmly, warmly into his. She holds it there and stares at him. The large blue Facebook icon glows.

"*Show me*," she whispers, and gets closer. "Show me your Facebook profile. *Please?*"

Jim and Randi, carrying file folders, dodge traffic and get to the center divider of the 22. Jim helps Randi climb over the guardrail, and they cross to the other side.

Seventy-five degrees.

"AAAAAAH! AH! AH! AH!"

Randi, naked, heaving, writhes on sheer, rumpled Motel 6 bed sheets. Jim, naked, is atop her, behind her, under her, over her.

"AAAH! AAH!"

Ultra-sensitive, Randi screams every time Jim touches her. The noise gives Jim a migraine. Randi pants and sweats, raking his back with nicotine-stained fingers. He coughs, exhausted, out of breath.

"*I can't believe,*" she yells as he thrusts from behind, "*you've never been on the Internet! That's so exciting!!*"

She screams again. Jim stares at a dusty painting on the motel room wall of Sioux warriors trying to kill an enormous bear.

Electronic Liquidators.

"Deer traps," says Louis Mohr.

"Deer traps?" says Jesus.

"Yes, where are the fuckin' deer traps?"

"The—the—"

"Want 'em big, but not too heavy. Y'know?"

"Deer traps?"

"Yes. Right."

"Don't sell deer traps," says Jesus.

"The hell you don't," says Louis, and he holds out the circular from the mail. "*Twenty-five percent off!*"

"Oh . . ." says Jesus. "Hold on."

He goes into The Nerd Cave and returns with a small, dusty, rectangular orange box, labeled DEER HUNTER PRO. He hands it to Louis.

"Cash or charge?" says Jesus.

"The hell is this?" says Louis.

"Just the game," says Jesus. "Gotta buy the gun separate. That's where they get you."

"*I got the gun*," says Louis.

"Great. Then you're set."

"I don't want this shit!" says Louis. "What else you got?"

"On sale? *Jewel Drop.*"

"You got traps? Nets? Camouflage?"

"Uh . . ." says Jesus.

"Explosives?"

"Uh," says Jesus.

Toi comes out.

"What's he need?" says Toi.

"Explosives and nets," says Jesus.

"Huh," says Toi.

Sixty-six degrees.

Motel 6.

Jim Chase, in blue slacks, blue socks, and blue Oxford shirt lies in fetal position on the bed.

"You should call the front desk," Randi says from the bathroom. "Your towels have holes."

She comes out dressed, prim and proper, picks up the maps and folders.

"Oh look! Look!" she says and goes to the window. She grins, gleefully, and heads out the front door.

Electronic Liquidators.

Louis Mohr comes out to the parking lot. Shrill honking grabs his attention. Traffic on the 22 has halted as a disoriented pack of white-tailed deer carefully leap the guardrail and cross the highway toward Electronic Liquidators.

"*Mother of God,*" whispers Louis.

On tiptoe, Louis darts to his pickup truck, reaches into the bed, withdraws his Ruger's 44 detachable rotary rifle, scurries to the edge of the 22, and kneels down.

Sixty degrees.

Motel 6.

"Jim! Jim!" says Randi. "Come outside! So pretty! And they're hardly—"

CRACK!

CRACK! CRACK!!

"Randi?" says Jim.

Jim comes out on to the Motel 6 parking lot. Randi lies in a pool of blood, a gaping gunshot wound in her left shoulder. Maps, folders and signed, authorized documents lie in a puddle of red ooze.

At the 22, blocked cars honk and sirens blare from a huddle of police cars. Over by Electronic Liquidators, uniformed policemen wrestle Louis Mohr to the ground.

Jim, shocked, kneels by Randi, his mouth agape. Peripherally, the untouched white-tailed deer lope past him through the Motel 6 parking lot, back toward the Watchung Mountains. But Jim doesn't see the deer because he has no peripheral vision.

Overlook Hospital. Emergency waiting room.

Fifty-four degrees.

Jim Chase sits in a worn, blocky wooden chair. His hair is in disarray. Large splotches of dried blood cake his shirt. He stares at the floor.

"Jim?"

He looks up. A short, stout, out-of-breath man in damp, gray sweat clothes stands over him. Jim looks up and sees him. The man grabs Jim's hand and shakes it, furiously.

"Thank you so much!" he says. "Thank you for bringing her in!"

"Sure," says Jim.

"You probably saved her life."

"I—"

"How's she doing?"

"She's—she's—who are you?" says Jim.

"Harvey," says Harvey.

Jim stares at him.

"Randi's husband," says Harvey.

Jim nods.

"Nice to meet you," says Jim.

Hospital hallway. Dan Morgan, the cop, and Kaye Mohr stand outside Louis Mohr's room. Inside the room, Louis Mohr sleeps, snoring loudly, his arm in a cast.

"He'll be fine," says Dan. "He'll get a psychiatric evaluation and they'll give him probation. Trust me, it could've been worse."

"He's not dangerous!" says Kaye.

Dan looks at her.

"Okay, when he's carrying a rifle, he's dangerous," says Kaye. "But that's over! He's just a crazy old man—he—"

"It's fine, Kaye," says Dan, pleasantly. "Don't worry. Everything'll be fine."

Kaye goes to the emergency waiting room and sits. She sits in a worn, blocky wooden chair, and stares, exhausted, at the dilapidated orange and brown carpet. Next to her sits Jim, exhausted, staring at the carpet. They both breathe, tired, numb. Jim doesn't see Kaye. And Kaye doesn't see Jim either.

And nothing else happens.

"What a fucked-up day," says Kaye.

Jim nods.

"I don't think a day can *get* more fucked-up," says Jim.

Jim turns to see who's speaking. And Kaye turns toward him. They see each other. And they both breathe slowly and turn back to the carpet.

And an orderly stops and looks up and out through the large, glass overhead ceiling.

"Mmh!" says the orderly. " 'Bout time!"

And Jim, Kaye, and the orderly stare up at the black, cool night sky and the beautiful, flickering white crystals pouring down upon them.

Snow.

Forty-one degrees.

Ace and Me

A BEAUTIFUL WINTER EVENING IN THE SUBURBS. HOUSES *everywhere glitter with holiday lights. JEFF walks his dog, ACE, late at night—the last walk before they turn in. It's freezing out, almost zero degrees and Jeff is shivering. Ace doesn't mind it quite so much and pokes his nose around, not sure what he wants to do yet.*

JEFF: Come on, Ace. It's freezing out here. Ace. Ace, please. Ace!

Ace finally looks at him, confused. Of course, they don't understand each other.

ACE: What?

JEFF: Just pee!

ACE: What?

JEFF: Just—tinkle! Come on! Tinkle! *Please.*

Ace looks around a bit, wanders around. He doesn't pee.

JEFF: Oh my God! Ace! Come on!

Ace looks at him.

ACE: What? What do you want me to do?

JEFF: Please, Ace! You're killing me!

ACE: What do you want?

JEFF: Tinkle!

ACE: What?

JEFF: Tinkle!

ACE: What?

JEFF: Tinkle!

ACE: Come again?

JEFF: Ahhhh!

ACE: I have absolutely no idea what you're talking about.

Jeff jumps up and down, panicked.

JEFF: Oh my god!

ACE: Can you just—hold that thought for one second—

Ace wanders over to the side and relieves himself. Jeff is ecstatic.

JEFF: Yes! Yes! Good boy! I knew we understood each other!

ACE: What?

Jeff reaches into a pocket, leans down and gives Ace a treat.

JEFF: Here's your treat!

Ace is ecstatic.

ACE: Thank you! Thank you!

JEFF: You're such a good listener!

ACE: I'm confused, but I love you.

The K-Rope

F AMED INVENTOR HARVARD KLEINMAN CAME OUT OF retirement Sunday to celebrate the seventieth anniversary of his illustrious K-Rope. At a special ceremony held at Newark Penn Station, Mayor Booker praised the apparatus, citing its historical impact on transportation in Newark, the United States, and across the globe.

While today's advanced K-Rope is well-known to the public, few may recall Kleinman's original device or even the inventor himself, for that matter.

"I was miserable," said Kleinman in a lengthy *Time* magazine interview, last year. "Before the rope, I didn't have two dimes to my name!"

The problem was simple: reduce the effort and wait times of rail commuters, who, in order to transfer from one train platform to a distant, parallel platform, had to descend a set of stairs, cross underground (in some cities above ground), and then climb a second set of stairs. Kleinman's solution: "The K-Rope"—a device enabling commuters to swing, Tarzan-like, across the chasm of rail-road tracks.

"Testing went on for months and there were some significant safety concerns," said Kleinman. "There was the problem of how to hold on to the rope so that anyone could do it, not just Johnny Weissmüller–types. You couldn't use straps because a person had to jump off quickly. Eventually, we came up with the lower plate for passengers to stand on. And then, of course, there was tim-ing of trains! Boy—we had close calls! We were very lucky in that all we ever suffered were scrapes and bruises. It was very much extremely dangerous work."

Kleinman's team worked exclusively at night. At first, they were forbidden from all testing because of the danger to trains and onlookers. Kleinman's angel came in the form of a 2 a.m. shift operator whose trains were already significantly staggered. Together, they worked without sanction of the Transit Authority. Had they been caught they would have likely suffered fines and possible jail time—an irony considering the inventor's initial rope-building inspiration.

"It was late summer, '41. I was coming home to New Brunswick—very late at night—and the platform was deserted. Suddenly, some two-bit thug, a turnstile jumper, bursts onto the platform, running crazy, followed by a couple transit police. The far end of the platform was gated—and this boy was completely trapped! Then he saw it. Dangling from the center girder, high above the tracks, was an old, abandoned construction chain with its tail end hooked onto the nearby platform wall. Without thinking, this kid unlatches the chain and leaps, swinging across the gap. *Unbelievable!* The police arrive a minute later, completely dumbfounded. *Where'd he go? Where'd he go?!* But *I* saw everything. The possibilities were endless! And that's when I got to work."

Of course, that boy, Ronald Snow, would come to plague Kleinman years later, claiming the rope had been his idea and demanding remunerations.

"He was a petty crook!" said Kleinman. "Nothing more. Threats, blackmail, lawsuits. And where did it get him? Leavenworth!"

In April of 1942, Kleinman's finished rope was formally presented to Mayor Vincent J. Murphy and the

Newark City Council. Kleinman declared that his device would reduce wait times, improve commuter traffic, and generate long-term revenues for the city. Then he presented the rope itself—a fine, thick, perfectly balanced blend of hybrid hemp fibers grown uniquely for their taut, superior strength.

"Harvey's designs were strict and exacting," said original rope team engineer Gerald Nowicki. "We could only use the specific fibers Harvey imported—strong enough to hold in excess of five hundred pounds—yet fluid enough to carry a man across a pit of seventy or eighty feet. We erected a series of pulleys, chains, and guide ropes, all carefully weighted and balanced. People think we just threw ropes up there! But Harvey was a mechanics whiz and his designs were flawless."

Following the technical presentations, Kleinman urged the mayor himself to test the rope. After a bit of nervous joking, Murphy stepped onto the copper standing plate, grabbed the rope, and leapt. Still famous today is the recording of his exuberant *"WAHOO!"* as he swung across the tracks. As each gray-clad councilman followed, their grimaces transforming to boyish grins, Kleinman knew he had a hit.

And what a hit it was!

That Christmas, K-Ropes were all the rage in Newark, and everyone who was anyone had to come take a swing. Gary Cooper, Greer Garson, William Bendix—even Boston slugger Ted Williams—all made pilgrimages to the station. James Cagney shouted, *"Top of the World, Ma!"* as he swung. Sixteen Radio City Music Hall Rockettes flew simultaneously—and as an unscheduled train came rattling in, no less! Santa Claus made an appearance, throwing gifts to children on both sides of the tracks. As it was war time, military men on leave were given passes to swing for free. The animated Bugs Bunny short *Bugs Takes a Swing!* garnered an Oscar nomination that season. And President Franklin Delano Roosevelt even sent personal notes to Kleinman and the mayor praising them for their innovation.

Tourism was at an all-time high. Train schedules were staggered to allow extra seconds for swingers to get "the biggest thrill ride of their lives." The public was so taken with K-Ropes they virtually stopped using them to commute and bought rail tickets just to take a swing.

"It was crazy," said Newark resident Joe Lamell. "A real mob scene. It got so crowded, you couldn't get on a platform, much less a train."

"We used to go every day," said former shop worker Alice Moore. "Just to watch! All those businesspeople—in coats and suits—swinging and screaming. And a minute later—*WHOOSH!*—trains whizzing by. I never did it myself. No. Proper girls did not swing on ropes. But you know . . . *I wanted to!*"

Demand grew rapidly. Ropes had to be replaced constantly because of wear and tear. Kleinman set up manufacturing operations to build and ship new ropes daily. And then came the competition.

"Z-Ropes! T-Ropes! Humdinger Swingers! They were all inferior ropes," said Nowicki. "You can't just make ropes and hope they work! Like making cars without brakes! Nobody bought any of them. All the stations stuck with Harvey."

Within two years, K-Ropes were installed across the nation in all applicable subway, bus, and railway stations. Schools taught K-Rope safety classes. And overseas, the devices were attracting attention on *both* sides of the war. Churchill was manic about installing them before Germany or Japan could, while the Axis powers were busy erecting poorly constructed ropes and meeting with catastrophic results. Starstruck, Kleinman abandoned his manufacturing plants and left for England.

And that was when the wasps came.

At first, it seemed a coincidence. A nondescript rail station in Indianapolis closed for a few hours one Sunday while several large wasps' nests were removed. But within a week all the nests had returned, plus a few dozen extra. Soon after, reports came in from across the nation of wasp infestations at train yards, and aggressive wasp attacks were being regularly recorded. Finally, the connection was made: *K-Ropes.*

It seemed the unique hemp fiber Kleinman had used was exceedingly attractive to a particular strain of Pepsis Formosa—or *Tarantula Hawk Wasp*—a species considered one of the most violent wasp families in existence. This unique strain had a dormancy period of approximately five years—the exact same time that Kleinman had created, tested, and installed his entire line of ropes.

By the time he learned of his mistake the damage had been done. Returning home from Europe, Kleinman faced public outrage, endless lawsuits, and likely bankruptcy. The media vilified him for leaving his home country during such a disaster. Kleinman begged policy-makers to let him redesign the rope and make amends. But it was too late. The public no longer wanted ropes fixed, they wanted them gone. After a historic three-year run, all K-Ropes nationwide were dismantled, removed, banished. Kleinman was a pariah.

Life on the railway lines went on. Tired commuters resumed walking down steps, crossing underground, and climbing a second set of steps when they needed to get to their far-off, parallel platforms. K-Ropes became a novelty; a sad, forgotten memory.

For the next two decades, Kleinman kept mostly to himself. For a while, he tried to find other applications for his pulleys and designs, but lawyers' fees and closing manufacturing plants ate up all of his finances. His one minor glory came late in the 1960s when his name appeared at the US Patent Office for an updated version of the Swiss Army knife. Kleinman had refitted the standard model knife with a tweezers and toothpick housed inside compartments. It was a quiet success with little media attention, and Kleinman returned to his seclusion.

And that would have been the end of Kleinman's story ... except for Bob Cross and Universal Dynamics.

In the summer of 2003, Cross announced production of a new, modernized K-Rope jumping off Kleinman's original designs. This new Smart Rope would be named the "K++" in honor of Kleinman. And the rest, as they say, *is history!*

Of course, you'd have to have been living in a Siberian cave for the last few years to not know of Bob Cross and Universal Dynamics. Most people know that today's Smart Ropes are constructed of zillions of micro-fibers that instantly conform to a user's unique body type and provide the exact lift or drag required. What you may not know is that each rope's nano-tech links directly to the nearest train station's grid, and instantly recalculates and adjusts for track switches and delays. Today's Smart Ropes give tired passengers a little extra push and have even dangled a person midair between two oncoming trains in one well-known, extremely hazardous incident!

And so, fans of the original K-Rope—of which there are *droves*—came out to Newark Sunday, despite the brisk, breezy weather. Mayor Booker ceremoniously unveiled the very first K-Rope (on loan from the US Transit Museum), which was in surprisingly good shape for a battered, seventy-year-old hunk of hemp fibers.

Finally, Kleinman himself stepped forward to give this wild new contraption a try. Though creaky in his step and suffering from arthritis, the inventor produced a clean bill of health from his physician and approached the K++ with anxious eyes.

"So, this is what they call a rope these days?!" said Kleinman to tumultuous cheers. His fingers clenched the rope as he stepped onto the molded Smart Plate which immediately resized itself to compensate for his weight and shoe size.

"*Nice!*" said Kleinman.

And then, he took a step back and made what can only be called a highly personal leap of faith. And millions of people around the world watched—on screens, phones, monitors and midair light shows—a moment of sheer grace: a brilliant octogenarian, frozen in midair and time, experiencing *utter glee*.

The Smoking Lounge

I AM THE FAT CHICK AND I LIVE IN THE SMOKING LOUNGE. It's the last day before Winter Break, snowing lightly, and I'm here in the Smoking Lounge, smoking. Skipping all my classes, having a good time of it. Funny that the school even has a Smoking Lounge. They don't have a "Getting Drunk" or a "Shooting Up" lounge. But they have this. My sweet little home away from home.

I am she-who-wields-the-Bic-lighter, and all know it. My best friend, Cathy, is here. Like me, Cathy is also grossly unpopular. She does, however, have a mouth like a garbage disposal: a plus in my eyes. She hates most everyone in the school and has been knocked up twice (that I'm aware of). Otherwise, she has the soul (and pipes) of an angel.

The Lounge itself is a tiny outside walkway cramped between the cafeteria and northeast entrance to the school. Snowcapped boulders, a wire-mesh garbage can, and white and tan crimped cigarette butts decorate its edges. The nearest wall is the back entrance of the gym.

And inside the gym the senior choir rehearses this year's Christmas concert. Pleasant, ambient choral sounds whisper from half-cracked-open windows atop the gym walls.

Cathy hates the choir and most seniors. Although she didn't even try out, she thinks Mr. Fleischer, the music teacher, should have personally driven to her house—in a limo—and invited her to join the choir. Of course, she would've said no. As much as she hates everyone, she also hates Mr. Fleischer.

Did I mention the tree?

Yes, there's a Christmas tree here in the Smoking Lounge.

"Where the fuck did that come from?"

"Dunno. I don't think it's the hall tree."

It's not as big as the one in the main hallway—or even as big as the three set up in the gym for the concert. But it's nicely decorated with lights and ornaments.

"Shit. Gives me the fuckin' creeps."

"A Christmas tree gives you the creeps?"

"Yeah. I don't get five fuckin' inches of this whole school, except for right here—and I don't need a fuckin' tree in my personal space."

"I think it's kind of nice."

"Well, shit, you would. You're into all that holiday festive bullshit! And I wish they'd STOP SINGING THAT FUCKIN' GODDAMN MUSIC!"

Abruptly the music stops. We look at each other, surprised.

"Now, that's service."

Dale, in an overcoat, with snare drum dangling from his neck, emerges from the gym door. He pulls out a pack of Marlboros, fumbles for a cig. I light him.

"Where'd you steal the tree from?"

"Who cares?" says Cathy.

"'Zat the one from the front hall?"

"It's smaller," I say.

"Kinda cool, just sittin' there," says Dale.

"Gives me the fuckin' creeps," says Cathy.

"This is her space," I say.

"Shit, it's everybody's space," says Dale.

"No—it's my space," says Cathy.

"Yer goofy," says Dale, throwing me a smile.

"Aren't you supposed to be practicing?" asks Cathy.

"Fleischer got one of his spastic coughing fits," says Dale.

Dale beats out "Little Drummer Boy" methodically on his drum, then hammers it into the solo at the end of

"Baba-O-Riley." Mr. Fleischer, still sputtering, pops his head out from the gym. Cathy and I hide our cigs. Dale throws his to the ground.

"Dale!" he calls. "Back in!"

Dale goes. Fleischer looks at the tree, at us.

"Is this one of mine?"

We stare at him, motionless.

"It had better not be one of mine!" he says, throwing a dirty look. And he disappears into the gym.

"Asswipe," says Cathy, pulling out a new cig. I light her.

"See?" she says. "They assume we stole the tree! Their tree! I can't even fuckin' breathe around here! Want some candy?"

She digs in her pocket and pulls out a Snickers bar. I shake my head. She eats.

I say no, but to be honest, I've got two bars in my left pocket. One partially ripped open. And I finger the chocolate, mindlessly, like a lucky rabbit's foot. I can feel the melted candy rubbing on my fingers and on the inside of my pocket, like greasy Playdoh or something. Better than eating it, right? I finger chocolate in one pocket, my lighter in the other. Ready for action.

Anyway, Cathy can afford the chocolate. She's got a few craters, but size-wise she's perfect. Certainly not forty-five pounds overweight, like some of us. What I have going for me: balance. I know myself, my limitations. I don't need to be "loved" by some creep on the football team, just to give myself some bullshit sense of self-worth. I can manufacture that all by myself.

Brit and Susie—neat, attractive seniors—come out of the cafeteria and pass through the lounge. They whisper and giggle and smirk as they pass us.

"Y'got a fuckin' problem?!" calls Cathy.

Brit wants to keep walking, but tan, lithe Susie comes back and stares little Cathy down.

"I only said one word," says Susie, holding up a single index finger. "Dirtbags."

Susie grins at Brit, who bites her lip. They turn—models on the catwalk—and wind down the path. Cathy burns.

"Fuck you! Y'fuckin' priss cunt bitch! Fuck your friends! Fuck your family! And fuck you, you fuckin'—"

"Nice tree!" calls Brit, and they disappear through the NE door.

Cathy attacks the tree; shakes it, kicks it, tears ornaments off and smashes them to the ground.

"Don't take it out on the tree—!"

"Shut up! Fuck you, Dutchy! Just—fuck you! Shit! Shit! Shit!"

And she disappears back into the cafeteria.

I step back, light up a new cig, take a lungful.

Did I mention that I've already lost three pounds?

No big deal. I've lost tremendous amounts of weight before. I can do it again. I just get sick of feeling this way, getting the looks. So, those are my gifts to myself this holiday: Willpower. An ounce of Grace. Peace on *my* Earth. (Good luck on yours.) And maybe a pair of black, big-ass Bose speakers.

Ms. Eiling, the guidance counselor, comes out for a smoke. She's thin, young, wiry, with weak eyes. But she's kind and doesn't condescend. She digs in her purse for a lighter. You know what I do.

"Thanks!" She laughs and we both smoke and stare at the tree.

"What a nice idea," she says. "Putting a tree out here. What are you doing for Christmas, Dutchy?"

"Nothing. Working. Staying home with the fosters. You?"

"Oh, nothing, nothing. Getting divorced." She laughs, embarrassed.

"Oh—I'm so sorry."

"No, no—it's a good thing. Long time coming."

She listens, quietly, breathes deep from her cig.

"What's the music?"

"Senior choir."

"Who's coughing? Fleischer?"

I nod.

"Poor guy."

"Mm."

She finishes her smoke, tosses her butt in the trash can. (First one today!) She smiles at me.

"Come see me in the new year, Dutchy!"

And as she heads in the NE door, Mr. Lymon, the school principal, comes out. I just manage to toss the butt behind me. He comes over, stares at the tree.

"Huh!" he says. "There really is a tree. How'd you get it out here?"

"Uhm. It was just here."

"Really? No idea where it came from?"

"No, sir."

"Hmm. Well, that's just plain we-eeird!" he says. "Don't you have class?"

"No, sir. Not for ten more minutes."

He studies me. Mr. Sherlock Holmes.

"Y'know, there's no smoking out here."

"Yes, sir. I know, sir."

"Good enough," he says, and disappears.

Maybe I should go in. Go home. Go somewhere. Anywhere.

A girl in whiteface comes out riding a unicycle. She wears black baggy pants and a white shirt with bright rainbow-colored suspenders. She cycles over to the tree and sizes it up. From behind her ear she withdraws a cigarette. She cycles over to me for a light. She nods appreciatively, smokes a bit, and then pulls out three red rubber balls and starts juggling. Unable to flick the cigarette, she alternately puffs and breathes while catching and throwing, catching and throwing. She catches the balls, puts two of them away. She arches her head so that her cig points straight up in the air—and then balances the third red ball perfectly atop the lit cigarette. She holds her arms out straight—and hovers—balancing the ball on the cigarette, herself on the unicycle. Ta da.

I clap.

She pops the ball off the cig, bows, throws the butt to the ground, and rolls over it back and forth with her unicycle. She spins in a circle and cycles off to the gym.

Cathy returns, all cleaned up. She pulls a cig out of her pocket. I light her.

"Shit. Sorry I said, 'fuck you,' Dutchy. Sorry."

"Jeez, Cathy. It's fine."

"No, no—I'm sorry. Just so stupid of me. I'm on a new fucking pill and I don't know—it's got me all fucked up. Sorry." She looks at me. "You lose weight?"

"Three pounds."

"No shit?!"

I smile.

"Dutchy! Good for you! Damn! You look great!"

"You want your Christmas present?"

"What? You didn't—sure—!"

"I'm wearing it."

"What?"

I remove the scarf from around my neck. It's long, textured wool. Itchy, uncomfortable. The way she likes it. She takes it, wraps it around her neck.

"Dutchy—shit—I didn't get you anything."

"*Please.* Merry Christmas."

Tears well in her eyes. She hugs me tightly. We step back, smoke, look at the tree. And I notice—it's so quiet.

"No more music," I say.

Cathy smiles, takes a deep lungful. And she starts to sing, almost in a whisper.

O Holy night, the stars are brightly shining
It is the night of our dear Savior's birth
Long lay the world in sin and error pining
'Till He appeared, and the soul felt His worth

With her gravelly, throaty, already-semi-ruined-by-cigarettes voice, Cathy actually can sing better—more fully—than probably anyone in the choir, maybe anyone in town. But rarely, rarely does she sing for other people.

The thrill of hope, the weary world rejoices

And the doors to the gym creak open and choir heads peer out, curious, surprised. They gesture to one another. Come out. Come out. In white, angelic robes—they watch this strange animal making strange sounds. Twenty of them, thirty, thirty-five. And Cathy's voice is loud now, vibrating, filling the air.

For yonder brings a new and glorious morn

Students, seniors, all classes, enemies, friends, people I've never met, teachers, Eiling, Fleischer, Lymon, all come out curious, listening, watching with the same wide-eyed wonder.

Fall on your knees

Oh, hear the angels' voices

Oh night divine

Oh night when Christ was born

And Cathy, enraptured in song, barely registers her audience—that her quiet, personal moment has grown into a bona fide concert, in our little dirtbag Lounge with our pathetic little tree.

Oh night divine

Oh night, Oh night divine

She wakes to the sounds of clapping, whistling, hooting, loud and thunderous.

"*Bravo! Bravo!*" shouts Mr. Fleischer.

Cathy smiles. But they don't stop. Surprised, she turns beet red, and waves to them like the Sweet Potato Queen.

"Alright! Back to class!" calls Lymon. "Everyone back to class!"

And almost everyone leaves. Mr. Fleischer hesitates, looks at Cathy—*sees her*—nods to her, approvingly. And then he disappears back into the gym.

And then it's just me and Cathy, and the lightly falling snow.

And we pull out new cigs. And I light us up.

"Let's make gingerbread," says Cathy. "Tonight."

"Okay," I say. "Let's."

Nick

*T*HE MIDDLE AGES. WINTER. A GENERAL STORE DECKED *out a bit for the holiday season. MACAWBER—a grungy, tired farm-keeper is purchasing goods from JANSEN, a slick, grungy storekeeper.*

MACAWBER: And give me a pound of feed.

Jansen reaches under the counter and withdraws a sack of feed.

JANSEN: Traveling?

MACAWBER: To Shepherd's Grazing.

JANSEN: Well! Six hours away! Staying the night?

MACAWBER: Not planning to.

JANSEN: And are you bringing *Nick*?

MACAWBER: Nick?

JANSEN: Well, y'can't take a trip these days without *Nick*!

MACAWBER: Mm.

Macawber is confused and uninterested. He starts to go. Jansen runs after him.

JANSEN: Let me describe something!

Macawber watches, dully.

JANSEN: It's late afternoon—you're tired. You've threshed the wheat—slaughtered the lamb. Yet, you've still got to travel four, five hours to Duck's Crossing.

MACAWBER: Shepherd's Grazing.

JANSEN: Over boring, tedious wilderness and countryside!

MACAWBER: I *like* boring countryside. It's soothing.

JANSEN: You only *think* you like it, because you never knew you had options! But now you have the *latest in traveler's technology!*

MACAWBER: (*confused*) Tech—?

JANSEN: Let me introduce you. (*calls*) Nick!

NICK, a gigantic lummox, steps out. He's dressed in tatters. He stands there, dumbly, nonmoving. Macawber stares, unimpressed.

MACAWBER: Who's 'is?

JANSEN: (*proudly*) *Thaaaaaaaat's Nick!*

MACAWBER: What's 'e do?

JANSEN: He orates.

Macawber is confused.

JANSEN: Speaks! Recites! Divulges—over a period of hours—stories of vigor, adventure, lust!

MACAWBER: Okay.

JANSEN: "The Curse of the Green Knight!" "The Lofty Handmaiden!" The *epic* "Tale of the Thieves!"

MACAWBER: Why would I talk to him?

JANSEN: You don't "talk" to him! He—

MACAWBER: I could talk to my wife.

JANSEN: Yes, but—

MACAWBER: I could talk to myself.

JANSEN: How about a simple demonstration? (*to Nick, waving a hand*) *Nick*—begin!

Nick speaks in a lummoxy, yet poetic and quite lyrical way. Macawber is impressed.

NICK: "It seems that I was traveling one brisk morning, when I happened upon a goat. 'Why, what a lovely goat' says I and happily—"

Jansen waves a hand and abruptly Nick stops. Macawber is on the edge of his seat.

MACAWBER: What was that!?

JANSEN: "The Lofty Handmaiden."

MACAWBER: Have him keep going.

JANSEN: Nick would *love* to keep going—

Macawber stares at Jansen.

MACAWBER: How much?

JANSEN: Quarter pig.

MACAWBER: Robbery! (*examines Nick, skeptically*) How's 'e work?

Jansen raises his hand, waves it, slightly.

JANSEN: Nick! Begin!

Nick starts telling a story.

JANSEN: He has volume control.

Jansen lowers his hand. Nick continues, whispering.

MACAWBER: What's he saying?

Jansen raises his hand. Nick continues, shouting.

MACAWBER: *TOO LOUD!*

JANSEN: Nick—stop.

Nick stops. Macawber stares at him, impressed.

JANSEN: Now, *you* try!

Macawber awkwardly raises his hand to conduct Nick.

MACAWBER: Nick—begin.

Nick starts telling a new story. Macawber raises his hand and lowers his hand, changing Nick's volume. He does a few sweeps. He does some quick jolts, trying to fake Nick out. Nick follows perfectly. Macawber brings him to a nice level and looks at Jansen, impressed.

MACAWBER: Nick—stop.

Nick stops. Macawber thinks, hesitates.

MACAWBER: Eighth of a pig.

JANSEN: Quarter pig.

MACAWBER: He's ugly.

JANSEN: You don't have to look at him.

MACAWBER: What if he falls out the carriage?

JANSEN: *Nick* comes with our brand-new, stream-lined, fiber security harness!

(He holds up a rope.) Free of charge!

MACAWBER: How do I know he won't—

JANSEN: What?

MACAWBER: You know. Club me and prod my wife?

Jansen withdraws a brochure.

JANSEN: Nick is guaranteed—!

He shows Macawber the brochure. Janson reads.

MACAWBER: ". . . won't club me or prod my wife—or my complete money back." Alright.

JANSEN: Listen, friend, take *Nick*. And if you're not completely satisfied, return him—free of charge!

Macawber laughs a dirty, grungy, seedy laugh.

MACAWBER: What if I *don't* return him?!

JANSEN: He'll kill you.

Macawber looks over at Nick. Nick nods. Macawber considers, gives in.

MACAWBER: Alright. Bill me the pig.

JANSEN: Very good! (*hands him rope*) Don't forget your security harness!

MACAWBER: (*to Nick*) Come on, then.

Nick hesitates. He trembles and begins to well up with tears.

JANSEN: *What?*

Nick runs to Jansen and hugs him, latching on tightly and crying.

NICK: *Don't want to go!*

JANSEN: Oh—you'll be back soon enough! *Go on!*

Jansen pries the crying Nick off and ushers him toward Macawber. Macawber and Nick exit. Jansen calls out after them.

JANSEN: And *don't* kill him!

Balance

THE TWITCH IS UNDER MY LEFT EYE.

The twitch is less pronounced right now, but it's there. Subtle. Sublime. Alive. Less noticeable. But there. A tic. A twitch. A muscle spasm. It floated around different parts of my body for a while, vacationing atop my right hand between thumb and forefinger, then surfing along various parts of my face before affixing itself—about a week and a half ago—to the fleshy curve beneath my left eye.

I recognize that it's hard to look at me with this twitch. It's not a blemish you can put makeup over. And because it's so *there*, front and center, tilting your head or giving a profile does nothing. You could wear sunglasses all day. But that's not a real solution. So, you try to relax and breathe and hope that when you have to face people, one-on-one, that your God is a loving compassionate God and that your eentsy facial tremors recede. Rarely though, do things work out so conveniently.

The twitch is a symptom of stress and exhaustion—specifically sleep deprivation. I've had insomnia regularly for a couple of months now. Sleep comes in spurts. I average about fourteen hours a week now and have only gotten an hour and a half over the last two days. I make some of it up on weekends. Sometimes. Sometimes I don't.

I've been out of work eighteen months now.

December 24th. One of the last working days of the year for people who are actually working. I'm in a meeting room at Mackinaw Kantor Insurance, waiting to be interviewed. The room is small, empty, not well lit. Interviewing is both my full-time job now and, approximately, an actual medical condition. The stresses and physical and financial deterioration, all the while trying to remain upbeat—*Upbeat!*—are like a terminal disease. But you get back out there, in clean suits, sleep deprived, buying cheaper, smaller cups of coffee, grabbing discarded copies of the *Times* after people leave them on train seats. You keep going.

A month ago, I waited over half an hour for an interview to start. The HR associate sat me in a glass cubicle dead center among the company's tightly packed workforce. She informed me that this cubicle had a phone and computer and if I wanted, I could get some work done. I didn't ask if he meant my own work or work for their company.

My phone vibrates. It's Matt. I shouldn't answer.

"Can't talk right now, Matt. It's a bad time."

On the other end, Matt whines.

"It is what it is," I say. "It doesn't concern you. Has absolutely nothing to do with you. Matt—I have to go."

I have what I call a "Balance List." It was my therapist's idea. It's a list of all the elements that make up my life: work, family, friends, sex, finances, spirituality, community, leisure, etc. I track this list every few days to see what's going well and improving, or stagnant and declining. I make tick marks and try to adjust my life as necessary. And all of this works toward keeping me, my life, everything, in balance.

Balance.

After a week's worth of tick marks, I review the list with my therapist to see if my adjustments are on target. But unfortunately, my Cobra ran out two months ago, and I haven't been to therapy since. So, now I just make adjustments randomly and hope for the best.

Oh, and for the record, Claire doesn't get benefits from the Hallmark store. So, currently, we have no insurance.

Anyway, about a year ago, to add some spiritual balance to my life I joined my friend Larry's local writer's workshop. We meet in people's living rooms and there's coffee and wine and hors d'oeuvres. Recently, I wrote a piece about a young man, Deke, who abandons everything—friends, family, material possessions—to wander the back roads of modern-day America. He sleeps in parks and bus stations and does odd jobs in bakeries and Chinese restaurants. He meets lots of girls, has unprotected sex, and searches across the nation for the perfect, slightly charred soft pretzel. Writing the story and reading it to the group was great, low-key, vulgar fun. And then about a week ago, I got tired of Deke and abruptly killed him off.

That's when the controversy started.

"You can't kill him off," said Matt. "It's inappropriate!"

Matt, a recent Rutgers grad, was a new member to the group. Before Matt, no one said anything substantial about anyone's stories. Mostly, it was "that's great!" or "that's sad!"

"What's inappropriate about it?" I asked.

"It's inconsistent with everything in the story," said Matt. "The tone. The pacing."

"It was pretty random in the first place," I said.

"People cared about Deke, Del! You didn't resolve anything. It was a sloppy, selfish way to end the story."

"So what?" I said.

That got him.

But Matt was determined. He called me at home—during the week—recruited other workshop members to stand with him. Then came the final insult—I started a new story.

This morning, on my train ride, Larry called.

"Matt's very upset, Del."

"So I hear."

"He's serious, Del. He's been sending emails. He's building support to have you kicked out of the group."

"You're kidding me?"

"Why don't you talk to him, Del?"

"Why?"

"He's upset."

"Son of a bitch."

"Anyway—"

"You agree with him?"

"No! Of course not. It's your story."

"Is anyone taking him seriously?"

"I have no idea. But—"

"But what?"

"Nothing. It's your business."

"That's right. And I hope what I do—what anybody does—with their pieces doesn't impact their standing in the group. It shouldn't."

"Of course not. He's just—he's very passionate."

"He's an idiot."

"It's nice that he cares so much about your work, Del. At least that's something."

The twitch has settled into a slow rhythmic pace, about one twitch every ten seconds or so, which is manageable. This kind of twitch could happen to anyone. Could be allergies. Not at all symptomatic of a manic sleep disorder.

I'm interviewing for a senior account officer position. I won't get the position. Or maybe I will. Maybe this will be my magic moment? I remain upbeat. *Upbeat!*

On the street this morning, I passed a young couple, kissing. Both were beautiful, New York bohemian types in their early twenties.

When I was in my early twenties I wanted superpowers—to fly or run fast or be strong or have super-vision. Now, I just want to be twenty. That, in and of itself, would be a superpower.

Another block down, I passed a man, stumbling, unkempt, with lesions all over his face. And I thought: *that's me, smack dab between the beautiful couple and the lesions.*

Balance.

"Clark Honeywell," says Clark Honeywell, triumphantly. His handshake grip is a vise.

"Del Sims," I return.

My interview starts.

Clark is an extremely well-dressed executive. Well-coiffed, his thick hair bristles. He has a hungry, focused look in his crystal-blue eyes. A man of power. About my age— maybe a little younger—but with the dynamism of a much younger man. He wears a crisp, well-tailored, gray pinstripe suit, starched white Oxford shirt, gold cufflinks, and tie clasp. And his tie is a smooth, muted burgundy with, at the bottom, tiny embossed golf clubs.

I wish I knew more about golf.

"Have a seat," says Clark.

My first thought is that Clark is a perfected version of me. Not just me in my Senior Title Officer heyday. No, Clark is an über-me; a me at hyper-velocities I can't even imagine. Clark looks like he, too, doesn't sleep much—but does much more productive things with his non-sleep time, like tripling his investments and sleeping with much, much younger women. Probably several at a time. Clark eats life. That's what he looks like.

What do I do with my non-sleep time? Lay awake, anxious, mostly; watch a little TV; try to get back to sleep.

I'm about two minutes into my modest career history—optimistically describing how my being imprisoned at the same insurance company for twenty-five years has given me the experiences and insight to conquer even the most technologically advanced, modern-day job—when I realize Clark isn't paying a bit of attention. He nods rapidly, corporately courteous, but his eyes continuously dart back to the meeting room door. And after two minutes—let's face it—it's too freaky not to mention.

"Are you expecting someone?" I ask.

"Sort of," says Clark. "So, how is it out there?"

"A little windy," I say.

He smirks, glances at the door again. Then he turns abruptly, leans close, and says, matter-of-factly:

"This is a really shitty place."

"Excuse me?"

"Del? Del, right?"

"Del."

"This place—Mackinaw Kantor—is a truly shitty, shitty, awful place."

"Okay."

"You don't want to work here. Trust me."

"You'd be surprised," I say, good-humoredly. "I've worked in some pretty shitty places!"

Clark stares at me, dead on.

"You worked at the same place for twenty-five years, Del?"

"Well. It had its shitty moments."

"Not like here. Trust me."

My twitch speeds up by about two seconds.

"Could we talk about the position?" I ask.

"Sure. What would you like to know?"

"Well, does it—is it—is the position—"

"The position, Del, is the exact same fucking thing you've done for your entire career. You're completely, perfectly qualified for it."

"Oh. Really?"

"Sure. Of course. Abso-fucking-lutely. Del, come on. You saw the description. What's to talk about? It's not a complicated position. Right?"

"Well."

He glances at my résumé. Not a look, a glance.

"You're dedicated, loyal, hard-working, committed, smart—*smart*—you are fucking smart, Del, right? A survivor! A self-starter. A game-player. Maybe not a leader of men—"

"Well—"

"Who cares?! It's not a leader of men position."

"So—"

"You're a consummate do-er, Del. Reliable. Trustworthy. You get the fucking job done."

"That's right."

"Anyone could trust you to finish. To deliver. That's what you do."

"Yes. That's right. I do."

"Y'know what? I'd be a reference for you, Del! I just met you two-fucking-minutes ago, and I'd be a reference!"

"Well. Great."

"And yet—with all these excellent credentials—you would still never ever *ever* get this job. And you know why?"

"I . . ."

"Because you're *too fucking old,* Del. That's why."

I say nothing. I breathe. Balance. Be calm.

"You are. That's the program. Sorry. How old are you? Sixty? Sixty-something?"

"Fifty-six."

"You look sixty-something."

"It's been a long year."

"I bet it fucking has."

And now Clark is up and looking out the door and coming back and leaning over the table.

"Makes no difference. You could be forty-five and you'd still be too fucking old. What you should do, Del, is go get a few stiff drinks, relax, and reflect on that great twenty-five-year gravy train you had. And I hope you invested well. Because today, you are fucked."

And that's it. For all I know this is illegal, unethical, something. But I make the professional gesture of checking my watch and pulling back my papers. And then Clark slaps his hand down on my résumé.

"What are you doing?" he asks.

"I—I have another interview at—"

"Really?"

"I—"

"Bullshit, Del. You don't have another interview."

"You seem like you're busy."

"Not at all. As a matter of fact—" and he gets up and looks out the door again. "I'm about to have an insane amount of free time. Honestly, Del—is this not the worst job interview you've ever had?"

"It's . . . pretty up there," I say.

"You should mention it to your recruiter. She—She?"

"She."

"She really fucked you this time."

"Clark," I ask. "Do you actually work here?"

"Up to about an hour ago, yes," he says. "Nice fuckin' Christmas present. *Merry Christmas, Clark. Don't let the fuckin' Giving Tree hit you on the way out!*"

"So—are you—are you hiding?"

"In a manner of speaking. I'm not a go-quietly-guy, Del. Not my nature."

"I would've guessed that."

The twitch recedes.

"Is it your nature?" Clark asks.

"I—yes, actually. It is. I would say I am—I was very much a go-quietly-guy. Yes."

"Mm."

"I—I had optimism then. Hope. I imagined that sweeping, tectonic changes in my life might actually—might actually be for the best."

"And what did that get you?"

"Twelve months of Cobra."

"And how long have you been out there, now? Knocking on shitty door after door after door?"

"Eighteen months and counting."

"Mother of fucking God."

"Yes."

"Still have hope?"

"I—"

And Clark actually looks at me. He shuts up and doesn't prepare to interrupt. For a few seconds, he simply listens, which was the highlight of my day, up to that point.

"Yes," I say. "Yes. I actually do have hope."

"Really?"

"Yes. Not much. A modicum."

"Huh."

"And that's about it."

"Well, you *are* a warrior."

"Thank you."

"Hate young people?"

"Excuse me?"

"I do. Fucking hate 'em. All of 'em! You hate young people?"

"I—sometimes. But I'm trying not to."

"I'm not. I hate 'em. I might not hate 'em tomorrow. But probably. That's who's taking my job, y'know?"

"Uh-huh."

"They actually admitted to me, this morning, that they had made this douchebag an offer. I'm not even out the door yet and they tell me this."

"That seems unprofessional. You might have a—"

"I don't have shit, Del. You know that, right? I don't have shit. Fifteen years. Four regimes. And y'know, I'd've done it, too. I *have* done it. Fired old guys. Not because they were old. *No, no!* Unproductive. Difference of opinion. *Bullshit.* They were old."

"Uh-huh."

"I mean, okay—but I don't look *that* old. Seriously. How old do I look?"

I make another polite watch glance.

"C'mon," he says. "Tell me. How old do I look?"

I shrug.

"Sixty?"

"Sixty?"

"Fifty-nine?"

"Fuck."

"How old are you?"

"Fifty-nine."

"It's been a real pleasure meeting you," I say and get up.

But Clark backs up hard against the door, blocking the only exit.

"Contrary to how this looks or feels, Del," he says, "this is not a hostage situation."

"O-kay."

"Do you know," he says, a far-off liquidy gaze in his eyes, "do you know what eight percent of all foreclosed homeowners do before they relinquish their homes? And, by the way, the eight percent is a New York state statistic, and frankly it's a few years old. I have no idea what the current national statistic is. But regarding eight percent of all recent New York foreclosed homeowners. You know what they do before they vacate?"

"I don't."

"And these, I add, are normal, natural, healthy, average, good, honest, middle-class, upper-middle-class people, Del. Not criminals or squatters. These are just good, decent, honest regular folks who have been, well . . . fucked. Fucked just beyond belief—all over the place. Eight percent. Thousands and thousands of people. You know what they do?"

"What?" I say.

And Clark takes a run at me. And I flinch, but quickly realize it's not me he's running at; it's the wall near me. And he bashes the right heel of his brilliant, shiny $300 wing-tip shoes squarely into the wall with the full force of a stocky 220-lb man. He kicks again and again. Malevolently. Mindlessly. Without rhythm or a beat. Again. Again. The plaster and paint crack. This mild, poorly lit meeting room that was just sitting here not bothering anyone. Again, he kicks, creating black scuff marks and holes in his futile rage. And the leather on his beautiful right shoe rips, his heel shredding to the point where he's kicking with his own heel—his flesh and blood heel—and he swivels and begins with the other foot, the other shoe, other heel. His fists clench, his face beet red. Clark is alive and goddammit he's not going quietly.

I watch for a second, surprised that no one, in all this time, has ever interrupted us. HR has not come to check on us or escort Clark quietly out of the office. Even now, with all the noise and ruckus, no one looks in. The holes will be replastered, repainted. Go ahead. Let him get whatever it is out of his system. Life goes on.

And in a few minutes, an hour, a week, Clark will start becoming me. Perhaps he already has.

I take advantage of the frenzy and slip out. As I head to the elevator bank, past cheerful receptionists, I hear the faint *thud-thud-thudding* of Clark's heel against the wall.

Down on the street, I feel cheated, stressed, sick. I have nowhere to go. So, I head downtown to Washington Square Park and do something I haven't done in thirty years, and what I do comes surprisingly natural to me. And then I head home.

On the train home, I call Matt.

"I've decided to rewrite the ending," I say. "I'm not going to kill Deke. Not yet, anyway."

"That's great!" says Matt. "That's really terrific."

"Thank you. Also, I've decided I'm going to leave the writing group. It's got nothing to do with you. Really. I just need to get my head together. Do less for a while. All for the best."

"I'm sorry to hear that," says Matt. "I think you've really got something."

"Thank you."

"I hope that when you finish the story, Del, you'll let me see how it turns out."

"Mm. No," I say. "I don't think so."

"Del?" says Claire, coming into the attic. "What's that smell?"

She looks at me in disbelief.

"Is that a joint?"

"It is," I say. "Want some?"

"No! What are you doing? At least open a window! Jesus!"

She waves at the air and opens a window.

"Claire—"

"What?"

"Please join me."

"No! Del—"

"Do you have any reason not to join me? Do you have anything better to do?"

"Of course!"

"Claire. Sit down and join me."

What I love most about Claire is her lack of resistance when there's no good reason to resist. At the moment, we had nowhere to be, no adult children to fret over, no urgent plans for the evening or morning or even the next day. There was simply no good reason not to smoke pot. So, we did.

Then with some stark, simple efforts, we undressed and made love and I won't bore you with the gory details. But it was pleasant and yes, we were overdue. And, look, if the pot enhanced the moment, then bravo for the pot.

Afterwards—several minutes afterwards actually— I found myself crying uncontrollably, like an eight-year-old.

"Del?"

"I lost money. I lost a lot of money—"

"Today?"

"No. Months ago. About a year ago—when this first started. When I got that first payout check."

"Del—"

"We had so much money, Claire. We had such a pay-day, suddenly, it didn't seem real. And I never play the markets. Never. And I thought, shit, what the hell, right? There was so much. And I did it. I put it in. The market fell *so* quickly. And I thought, *hey, it's just a fluke. It fell, so, now's the time to buy!* Right? And I put *more* in, Claire. *More!* Like an idiot—I had no idea what I was doing. I wasn't—I couldn't think this far ahead—"

"How much?"

"From—from—"

"Total. Beginning to end."

"Thirty thousand."

"Huh."

"Thirty thousand. Thirty thousand—and then I moved it all back into bonds and money markets. And I lied and told you that we made less than I originally thought. I—I fucked it all up, Claire! Thirty thousand dollars—"

"It doesn't matter, Del. You thought it was best at the time. You were trying to make something work."

"I'm not a gambler."

"Del. *Shh.* Everything's fine."

"I—"

"I know."

"I'm so sorry, Claire. I'm so sorry about everything."

"I know. I know. I forgive you, Del. It doesn't matter. It really doesn't matter. You meant well."

"I love you."

"I love you, too."

And I sleep. Eight hours. Ten hours. Fourteen. I sleep, solid. The sleep of a child.

When I wake the next day—

Christmas morning.

And the twitch is gone.

For now.

Her Day Off

S HE SAT AND SAT. AND THEN THAT WAS ABOUT ENOUGH. She let her book fall onto the table, stood, stretched, left the room, left the house. The world outside was tremendous.

The crisp coolness, the beauty of the fresh fallen snow, the smell of pine needles, of the season itself—of winter— overwhelmed her. A perfect day to shake out the cobwebs, she thought; to realign herself; to walk into town. Certainly, much too perfect to be cooped-up indoors.

So many choices. She'd seen a delicate ruby brooch at the Jumble Store that had really caught her eye, and she considered spoiling herself and getting chocolate. But instead, she settled for a simple bag lunch in the park. She stopped at the butcher's, picked up an oversized bag of popcorn, a large cocoa (*what the hell!*) and—as a special treat—a quarter pound of chipped ham which she might possibly eat with her fingers, girlishly and uncivilized, straight out of the wrapper.

The park, with its glistening frozen-over lake, was bliss. She picked a clean, warm-looking bench. And except for a few dog-walkers, she had the place to herself. Now, she would let go of time and burdens and live in the moment, enjoying simple listless currents. Today, the absence of time was her friend.

Slowly, messily, she ate and drank. She watched a family of geese effortlessly dive and swoop. She drank in every wisp of breeze, and the welcoming warmth of the midday sun. If you asked, she'd swear she heard every sound nature could make that afternoon. Maybe she'd even throw popcorn to the geese, despite all the signs warning against it.

A quarter of the lake away she saw a young man, a lone skater, gracefully gliding and spinning, as if performing a routine solely for her pleasure. She wanted to applaud him and wondered if he even noticed her there on the bench. Instead, she kept quiet and marveled at his slow and steady effort, his patience, his polish.

She wanted to meet him suddenly and skate beside him. She wanted to join this kindred spirit and become one forever with all this glorious natural beauty, even though she could barely stand on skates. She would go over, she decided, and introduce herself. And he'd be pleasant and friendly, and they'd easily get along.

And she was restless, suddenly. Obligations, unfinished chores, filled her head like a cloud of gnats. She closed her eyes, took a breath, and released them all back to the ether. But when she looked again it was too late.

The moment was gone.

When she returned six hours later, it was still early, still a long time before Mrs. Cooke would be home from work.

The TV was on. As expected, the old man was on the floor. He had messed himself, and was wheezing and whimpering, his arms trembling slightly from side to side. One of his oxygen tubes had dislodged but he was fine. He was still getting more than enough air. What did it matter, anyway? He barely knew where he was.

She changed his sheets, threw them in the wash, then cleaned and changed him as well. She lifted him back into the bed, noticing that he seemed lighter today.

After a few minutes, as his disorientation and panic subsided, he lolled off and went back to peaceful, peaceful sleep.

She sat back down in her chair and picked back up her book.

And she read.

Young, Confused Parents

A basement playroom. ELLEN, 35, sits on the floor tightly holding her infant son, KEVIN, who is trying to crawl away from her. Across the room from them crouches her husband, DAVID, 36, who holds a large flat piece of matzah.

ELLEN: Ready?

DAVID: Let him go!

Ellen lets Kevin go. She darts across the room, crouches a few feet away from David and holds out a wafer. Kevin crawls hesitantly, slowly down the middle.

ELLEN: *Here, honey!*

DAVID: *This way, Kev! C'mon! Come to the matzah!*

ELLEN: *Come on, honey! Body of Christ! Come to Mommy!*

DAVID: *State of Israel, Kev! Zion!*

KEVIN: (confused) Eh—Ah—?

Ellen's cell phone rings.

ELLEN: Time!

Ellen pulls the phone out of her back pocket, gets up and paces around. David picks up Kevin.

ELLEN: (into phone) Hi, Mom. Yeah, he's picking his religion, now. Fifty bucks on the church? You got it!

David sneaks a piece of fruit to Kevin. Ellen notices.

DAVID: (whispers) And there's *more* where that came from—!

ELLEN: What are you doing?

David quickly burps him.

DAVID: Gas!

KEV: Hah?

Ellen continues on phone, pulls out a notepad, makes notations.

ELLEN: Alright, Ma. No, it's just paying even odds at the moment. Right. We'll let you know.

She hangs up. David replaces Kevin at the starting spot, gets him in crawling position.

DAVID: (to Ellen) Ready?

ELLEN: Let's do it!

David lets go of Kevin and runs back to his place next to Ellen. They continue yelling at Kevin, who creeps along, confused. They are much more frantic this time.

ELLEN: *Come on, baby!*

DAVID: *Move, Kevin, move!*

CHLOE, their twelve-year-old HARI KRISHNA daughter comes in, wearing robes.

CHLOE: Krishna, Mom. Hari Hari, Pop.

DAVID: *Off-side!*

ELLEN: Chloe—you're standing in the playing field!

CHLOE: Don't you guys think—Rama Rama—maybe there's a better way to do this?

DAVID: What? You mean use the *Spinning Wheel 'O Religion* again?

ELLEN: Like we did with you?

DAVID: I mean—that thing is *way* in the back of the garage!

CHLOE: Hari no, Dad! But Krishna, sometimes I think—what if *my* wheel had come up Amish or

Baptist
or—or—or—or—or—or—or—Zoroastrian?

David goes and plays with Kevin.

ELLEN: We never wanted to force our beliefs or
our parents' beliefs on you, Chloe. We wanted to be
completely impartial!

David shows Kevin how good matzah is to eat.

DAVID: Isn't matzah good? Mmm! Yes, it is!

CHLOE: Did you ever think that maybe—I
dunno—you and Dad were projecting your utter
lack of spiritual faith on to me and Kevin?

Ellen's cell phone rings. She pulls it out of her back pocket.

ELLEN: (to Chloe) Hold that thought. (to phone)
Faith Race! Can I—Gillian!? Of course! Absolutely!
(to David) Carters put twenty on the Church!

She hangs up. Chloe steps between them.

CHLOE: Okay—here's an idea! Why don't you expose Kevin to Judaism *and* Catholicism slowly as he grows up, and let him come to the choice organically on his own?

David and Ellen consider this. Long beat.

ELLEN: Wow. That could be really tiring.

DAVID: Honey—we thought *a lot* about what we're doing. And this is *so* much easier.

ELLEN: Just decide his faith and move on!

DAVID: (checking his watch) Guys—I've got a game at six and we still have to determine his career and political slant.

CHLOE: What about his sexual preference?

ELLEN: (laughs) That's next week.

CHLOE: Alright. Can I at least call the play-by-play for my friends?

She pulls out her cell phone and aims the camera at Kevin as David sets him up again.

ELLEN: Of course!

David lets go of Kevin and runs back to his place next to Ellen. The tableau repeats. Chloe films with her phone and calls the play-by-play. Slowly, awkwardly, Kevin makes his way toward his parents.

CHLOE: (in elevated announcer's voice)
Annnnnnnd he's crawling down the center of the field! This is tremendous! The determination on this child's face! What must be going through his mind? A lifetime of Novenum? Or merely: *Hungry. Want num-num.*

Kevin gets to the far end but hesitates between his mother and father. He can't choose.

CHLOE: Annnnnnnd—he's torn! Judaism! Catholicism! Judaism! Catholicism!

Kevin reaches for his father.

CHLOE: It's Judaism! Judaism! What a day this is for the chosen people!

David leaps up, holding Kevin and screaming.

DAVID: *YES! YES! MY BOY! WAY TO BE!*

Chloe goes to interview David.

CHLOE: Dad—can you tell everyone how it feels to be father to a new member of the tribe of Israel?

DAVID: Feels good—*good!* We wanted this bad! And we worked for it!

Chloe goes to interview Ellen, who looks downtrodden.

CHLOE: Mom—this isn't the first of your offspring to fall by the wayside biblically speaking. How does it feel, knowing yet *another* child may not make it to the Kingdom of Heaven?

ELLEN: *It—it frickin' sucks!!*

CHLOE: Will you have another child and try again next season?

Ellen stares tearfully at David. David stops reveling and watches her.

ELLEN: I—I—I—I just don't know.

David goes to her. His head hangs in guilt.

DAVID: Honey. I have a confession to make. I—I wanted Kevin to be Jewish so bad—I rubbed peach Gerbers all over myself this morning. I'm *so* sorry.

She looks at him, also filled with guilt.

ELLEN: I've got a confession, too, honey. Yesterday, while you were at the Mets game—I had him baptized.

They stare at each other, full of shame.

DAVID: Honey, maybe Chloe's right? Maybe we should take Kevin to temple *and* church and let him make up his own mind as he gets older? Maybe we should be the kind of loving, supportive middle-American family you just don't see anymore?

They all embrace with Kevin in their arms, joyfully.

ELLEN: Oh—honey—now I *know* we'll be the best parents ever!

DAVID: You're the best, babe!

ELLEN: No, *you!*

They look at each other, warmly.

DAVID: Hey! Let's race Kevin to see who he loves the most!

ELLEN: *You're on!*

Brownie Mix

I'M CLEANING THE KITCHEN. EVERYONE'S GONE NOW. THE sink is full of dishes. The floor is sticky. The garbage is full. The oven and stovetop are a mess. Food's rotting in the fridge. Everyone's gone. Gone home. Gone to hotels. Gone to the airport. Annie and Jake and Tom are upstairs, asleep. I'm alone. It's snowing outside. That's okay. I don't mind cleaning up. This is the first privacy I've gotten in days. The only privacy I ever seem to get anymore. Cleaning the kitchen. Mm. That's fine. That's fine. There are spilt coffee grinds on the floor. What a mess.

Are we out of sponges? Where did she put the sponge? She never replaces the sponge. She throws it out and doesn't put a new one back. What? Am I the only one who lives here? No, there are more sponges in the cabinet. Fine. Fine. No, I need the kind with the abrasive side. Okay. There it is. Good. Look at this stove. This gravy is dried on here. It's like a crust—a burnt crust. Okay. Just takes a little elbow grease.

How long have I been cleaning the kitchen? I never used to clean the kitchen. I actually like cleaning the kitchen. I don't remember ever cleaning the kitchen before we were married. Before we bought the house. I never cleaned a kitchen in my twenties. Who cleaned the kitchen back then? I must've. Or my roommates? Maybe there weren't dishes back then? Maybe we just threw everything out. Or maybe I just cleaned less frequently? Once a month, maybe. When the sink was full. I don't remember ever taking out trash. Only when it was absolutely necessary. Now, I clean the kitchen, take out the trash, nightly. I live in the kitchen, cleaning the kitchen. I don't mind it. Really. It's okay. It's peaceful. It's like meditation. Some people go to the gym—go to therapy. I do dishes. Mop. Scour the stovetop. Change the utility light bulbs. Clean out the fridge.

Annie and the boys are upstairs, asleep. They conked out early. They always do. She falls asleep with them, gets up, moves into her own bed. Our bed. I'm left with the kitchen. Alone. Alone. Alone.

I have a dishwasher—but I only use it to wash the acceptable dishwasher dishes. The rest of them I do by hand. Save on my water bill. I've seen the dishwasher ruin things before. Melt Tupperware. Of all the dishes to be washed, I'd say 30 percent of them end up in the dishwasher. I realize that I should—I *could* probably trust it with at least 10–20 percent more dishes—that I need to delegate more to the dishwasher—but I dunno. I don't mind doing the dishes. I use gloves. Rubbermaid. (Of course.) The kind with the soft latex inside. Especially in the winter, now. Hands cracking and chafing. For the amount of water and dryness I get exposed to—I have to use gloves. So, that's fine.

Look at the sink! I've got to scour and clean the sink now. Like cleaning a bathtub. You wouldn't *not* clean the bathtub every couple of days, right? Of course not. Anyway, it just takes a minute. And this floor. God, look at it. You can barely walk. It's like stepping on a bed of gum. What is this—a saloon? Too many people—in and out. No respect. I'll mop. Well, I've gotta sweep first. Well, really—I should clean the table first, before I sweep. And the chairs. If I'm going to do the floor—I should wipe off the table and chairs. Shake out the placemats—into the sink and trash. And—*mf*—there goes the sink again! Well, I can just rinse it and that's fine.

Didn't this used to be women's work? Wasn't the kitchen the woman's—the wife's domain? When did that change? Or did it change? Maybe it's me. Maybe I'm the wife? When did I become the wife?

Hm. I could leave it. I could stop. No one's forcing me to clean the kitchen. There's no time limit here—what with everyone upstairs, asleep. But I have to finish. I mean, sooner or later. I can't just leave it. And it is getting clean. There's a sense of ownership, pride—to a clean kitchen. A job well done. Even though I know I'll be back tomorrow—starting all over again. There's still a sense of peacefulness that you made it presentable. That's the real way to end the night—a sense of balance.

A fire engine goes by outside. Sirens blaring. Red lights flashing. Down the end of the street and turns. A police car follows, flashing lights waking up the night. All our neighbors have their holiday lights up. Elaborate stuff. We didn't get invited to any parties this year. Just as well. Who has time? Who has the energy?

Tonight was supposed to be Movie Night. We set aside one night a week to put the kids to bed and then cuddle up, watch a movie. Just the two of us. But she always falls asleep putting the kids to bed and I end up cleaning the kitchen. Actually, we've never made it to Movie Night. We've rented a lot of movies. We tend to rent the same ones over and over and over—since we never watch any of them. It would probably be a better investment to buy the movies, instead of re-renting them every week. But they'd just accumulate, unwatched. At least this way, we save space. We could just stop renting movies altogether and put Movie Night on hiatus, till the kids grow up. But that seems too resigned. I mean, if *she* wants to give up on Movie Night, fine. But I'm certainly not going to. If I suggested it, God, what would *that* mean? Hm.

I'm scrubbing, scouring the stovetop. My ulcer doesn't bother me as much as it used to. You have to scrape and scrape with the abrasive side of the sponge to really get it up. But it comes. Most of it. You think you're gonna scrape right through the metal. Scratch it. But you don't. Whoever made these abrasive sponges knew what they were doing! They knew just how much abrasion you need to get off the grime without hurting the stovetop. Good stuff.

I put on some music. Kitchen cleaning music. Haydn. Strings. Mellow. Very nice.

Hmm. Sounds like there're animals in the garbage outside. Squirrels, raccoons, skunks.

What we should really do is remodel. Then it would be new. New! All the time new! For a while anyway. I mean I'd have to keep it new. I'd have to work at it. Clean it, basically. Probably have to clean it more. If I'm going to invest all that money—I'd want to keep it spic and snappy. Not like this old piece of crap. Not that this is a piece of crap! This is family.

Maybe I'll make some fresh coffee. There's a burnt brown film on the pot. She just leaves it there all day. I guess she—what? Rinses it? Throws out the old grinds, adds new grinds, water. I could make a fresh, *clean* pot. No. It's too late. It'd just keep me up all night. Decaf? Or tea? A nice herbal, holiday spiced tea, maybe? Hm.

Well, what if I stopped cleaning the kitchen? What if I said, "Damn the kitchen! To hell with the kitchen!!" What would happen? Would the police come? Would the Earth open up and swallow me? I'll tell you what would happen: the kitchen would be a mess. Well, big deal! Do I own the kitchen or does the kitchen own me?

I've had a lot of urges to cry lately.

I cheated on Annie three years ago. No big deal. It was no big deal. Brief. Very short-lived. Only what—a few weeks—maybe a month and a half? Meaningless. Don't even know why I did it, really. I wouldn't do it again. That's for sure. I wonder if we have brownie mix?

Annie found out. (How could she not?) She wanted to leave me. Wanted to leave and take the kids. She didn't. She stayed for the boys' sake. For the family. Didn't mean anything, anyway. It was years ago, now. Moment of temporary—what—insanity? Long past. And now—what—she's upstairs with the kids—upstairs, asleep. Everything repaired. Back to normal.

There's some kind of dried something—fruit?—on the floor in front of the stove. So, I will have to mop. Hm. Out of paper towels.

And X? Long gone. Long, long gone. Who knows where she is? Who cares? What a waste. Not worth it. Not worth it for the five minutes of whatever it was— for the endless ramifications it would have on my—on my life. Hmm. Ramifications? No. No ramifications— nothing long-term, anyway. Everything's fine. Everyone's fine.

Lunchboxes. Can't put 'em in the dishwasher. Have to clean 'em by hand. Of course. Of course. Have to clean out the fridge before bed. Well, obviously, I have to clean out the fridge!

It was right after Tom was born. It just happened. I dunno. I was very out of control. Exhilarated. The highs and lows. I would feel alternately euphoric—a virile kid— and then the shame, the guilt, the fear, the absolute dread of losing everything important to me for this momentary, meaningless—thing. The panic. I'm surprised it went on for as long as it did—which was only weeks. Maybe a month and a half. I was not a good liar. Especially considering that I had put our entire family in jeopardy. I was simply too sick about it. Losing too much sleep. And, of course, Annie knew. She knew and wouldn't let me rest until I confessed it all. I shouldn't've. I should've held my ground. But I was—what? Weak? No. How could I have held it in? How could I? I was beside myself. I punished myself far more than she ever could have. Although, she certainly gave it the old college try.

My smashed thumbnail has practically grown out. Doesn't look too bad. Maybe I'll make turkey tacos tomorrow!

I moved out. Lived at the Sheraton for three months. I told her it was over. (By the time she found out it had been *long* over.) After moving back in I slept in the spare room. Slept there for a year by myself. Alone. Alone. If Tom hadn't been so young, I might not have gotten back in the house at all. But Annie needed the help. She needed help and she loved me. And she hated me.

Her father died, after a year. And I was there.

It's the past. Long gone. Everyone's okay. Fine. Everyone's healthy. Money in the bank. The kids are okay. Everyone's upstairs, asleep. Asleep, peaceful—as the holiday ends and the snow falls. She loves me again. Needs me again. Trusts me. I'm useful to her again.

Do I want to clean the kitchen? Of course not. Do I like cleaning the kitchen? Of course not. Who wants to clean the kitchen?! But it's got to be cleaned. Somebody's got to clean it. The kids aren't old enough to clean it. Yet. So, do I want to? Do I like to? Do I enjoy it? No. But I do it. Which, of course, is fine. Really. Really. That spot on the stovetop. It's like—paint—dripped from the ceiling.

Okay—let's try a little boiling water—here we go— here we go—just wipe away—and—oh my God! Oh my God! I scratched it! I scratched the metal! Goddamn it! Good goddamn it!

God, I'm just. I'm stressed. To bed. I should get to bed. With my wife. They'll be up at dawn. They always are. I need sleep. Staying up playing games with myself. It's crazy. I'm crazy. An idiot. Standing here—cleaning the kitchen. What an emotional cretin. I have nothing to complain about. Nothing. I'm lucky. I'm in a good place. Everything is calm, peaceful, balanced. Nothing to complain about. The goddamn luckiest man on Earth. That's what I am. Lucky. Content. Cleaning the kitchen. Still have to bag the trash. Double-bag it. There. Gotta put a new trash bag in. Hm. Gotta remember to—what?—run the dishwasher before I go up.

Look at it. Look at it. Still coming down. Heavier than ever now. Wasted. All this—magnificence—wasted on me.

Teapot's hot. Made a cup of cocoa. God, I'll have to shovel tomorrow. All day if it keeps up.

I sit. Stare out the window. Falling. Falling. Everything's quiet. I'm sitting. Staring out the window. Sipping cocoa.

And everyone's upstairs.

Asleep.

Julian

I'M STANDING ABOVE THE BATHTUB. THE BATHTUB'S FULL, the water clear, cold. But I'm not getting in.

Above the water, I hold a thick, 180-page notebook with a worn blue cover. The notebook is almost completely full of words. On some of the pages the writing is so dense that there are multiple lines within lines, regardless of where the college rules are. On some pages there are only a few words, but they are gigantic, and say things like *this sucks*, and *what am I doing? I have no idea what I'm doing anymore*. The words are almost all uniformly in caps; some written in a swirly scrawl, others with the appearance of being traced over and over as if to emphasize seriousness, anguish, conviction.

This is my journal of the previous year.

I fan the pages above the water like an accordion, shaking it to more effectively loosen each page from the others. That way, all pages will be exposed, and at their most vulnerable when I drop the notebook in the water.

"I've brought you a gift," says Julian.

He steps into the apartment and two young women follow in after him. They are—not bad-looking, I guess. Odd? Homely? Perhaps European? Appalachian? Hard to tell. Clearly from out of town. Both are blonde, early twenties, sort of cute-ish, in need of orthodontia.

Julian, in round glasses, rainbow scarf, shoulder-length woolen cap, purple thermal shirt, ripped jeans, and a ratty overcoat, looks like a cross between an elf, a Haight-Ashbury hippie, and a holy man. The girls are dressed similarly—in colorful, woolen caps with ear-side tassels to their waists, ratty coats, ripped jeans. Both look lost—like they hitchhiked here, looking for adventure. What they found was Julian.

"Lisette, Becca—this is Seth," says Julian.

"Hullo," they say.

"Uh. Hi," I say.

And they walk in and look around.

Julian himself only arrived from Boston earlier this morning. We've known each other since we were tots growing up in Milwaukee. We were those kids whose parents were friends, so they stuck you together and hoped for the best. But with Julian it was different. He had only a few close friends—and would go through periods where he would call me every day, a playmate to get in trouble with.

When he was about ten, two significant things happened to him: his father died, forcing his mother to move the family to an apartment across town; and he discovered he had an innate talent for drawing exquisitely detailed biblical-cum-pagan pen-and-ink grotesqueries which became his lifelong passion. Over summers, he was generous with his art, even giving me a rapidograph, which I still have dried-up in a box to this day. At eighteen, he went to art school in Boston, apprenticed for C-level artists, and began transforming his own ideas into oils, metal, sculpture.

"I don't need a gift," I say.

"Course you do. C'mon, get your stuff. Let's go."

"Where are we going?"

"I dunno. Guess we'll find out when we get there. By the way—you have any pot?"

"No."

The girls giggle, confused.

"I promised weed!" He turns to them. "That's why they're here. So, we must find some!"

Lisette raises a hand.

"I have to pee," she says in broken English.

I point to the tiny bathroom, and both girls go in. Julian looks at me, his eyes wild.

"Who are they?" I ask.

"Dunno. Just found 'em."

"Where—?"

"In a line buying hot dogs, up at Third—"

"You found them in a line getting hot dogs?"

"They're not from around here I don't think."

"Where are they from?"

He shrugs.

"Sweden or maybe Kentucky. I really have no idea. Who cares?! They're extremely friendly."

"Uhm."

"Which one do you want?"

"Neither."

"Well, you have to pick. That's my Christmas gift. I found them. So, you get to pick."

"I don't want a Christmas gift."

"If you don't pick—I pick—and I already have an opinion!"

"And—what do you want to do with them?"

"What do I—?" He grins. "I'm open to suggestion."

"I'm going to stay here," I say. "I'm in the middle of something."

"What? This? Are you at a critical juncture?" he goads.

I sit among dozens of papers with little color-coded marks all over them. Sheets and sheets of a terrible screenplay that's going nowhere, but that I feel extremely committed to. Or maybe I'm hiding behind it, I wonder.

The girls come out of the bathroom, beers in hand, grinning.

"Who's ready for exploring?" yells Julian.

"Whoo-hoo!" they say, waving their beers, unsure what's going on.

"Friendly!" Julian announces. "I like it!"

Julian darts out into the hallway. The girls follow after him, and now, I figure, might be a good time to try Terri again. But I get her message for the fourth time today and hang up.

Out in the hallway, I hear Julian knocking on my neighbors' doors, several at a time. I look into the hallway as he's asking an elderly, half-asleep Greek woman: *Have any pot? No?! Anyone else inside there?* She slams the door on him, but he's already knocking on other doors. *Got any pot? Any pot for me?*

The girls giggle, loiter. I grab him.

"These are my neighbors!"

"Well, somebody's gotta have some. Shall we try the crack house, then——?"

"No!"

For the decades I've known Julian, I've envied his wildness, charisma, artistry, freedom, good looks, and knack for getting away with everything. In fact, I consider myself, essentially, dull around him. As far as I know Julian has only ever envied one thing of mine: my apartment.

My apartment is an awful, awful apartment. With crumbling walls, bugs, faulty heating, occasional rats, and no upkeep whatsoever by the landlord, it is easily the worst place I've ever lived in my life. It is tiny, meager. A Hobbit would feel cramped in this apartment. And for this luxury palace I pay almost two thousand a month which—as a paycheck-to-paycheck temp worker—I can never quite afford.

But this shameful, unsafe apartment—which by the way is located upstairs from a ramshackle tattoo parlor fronting for an actual crack house with actual junkies lying on the stoop every day—just happens to be located at 8th

Street and 2nd Avenue—an area in the East Village commonly known as Saint Mark's Place.

So, it's a shithole, but—to folks like Julian—a shithole in the Center of the Universe.

Washington Square Park.

The park is crowded with huge, lit-up Christmas wreathes, people colorfully dressed, and competing musicians playing dissonant carols on violins, guitars. There's a chaotic festiveness to the atmosphere which we drink up. It's not the Christmas of my youth. But then it hasn't been that for a while now.

Julian confers with several drug dealers, sniffing wares, demanding samples, negotiating prices. He thinks he's in a terrific movie about himself, but his elfin charm is lost on the locals. He's too bright and shiny.

He returns to me, energetically.

"Got forty?"

I give him money and a minute later we're all huddled on a bench lighting up. The girls pass joints and are excited again. And a thick, but not windy, snow begins to fall.

"I love Christmas in New York!" shouts Julian, jumping up, opening his mouth and catching the snow. The

girls joyfully mimic him, and he reaches out to Lisette—
the taller, ganglier one—and kisses her. She pulls back,
surprised, but then gives in and lets him. Becca looks curiously at me. But all I can muster is an embarrassed, frosty
breath.

"Where are you from?" I ask, gently.

She stares at me, confused.

"English?" I say. "Sprechen sie—English?"

"Uh—uh—no—" she says and holds up fingers indi-
cating "just a little."

"Europe?" I ask. "Germany? Sweden?"

She shakes her head.

"Utrecht," she says.

Utrecht? My geography for the East Coast alone
sucks. I have no idea where Utrecht is.

"Netherlands," she says.

"Oh. Oh," I say. "Norway? Norwegian Wood?"

She looks at me, confused, tries to think of something
else, comes up short.

"Netherlands," she repeats. She points at me. "New
York?"

"I—well, now—I guess. Not always," I say.
"Milwaukee."

"Milwaukee?" she repeats, smiling. And I suppose, to
her, I just said "Utrecht."

"Old Milwaukee!" says Lisette, waving her beer bottle.

"Ah—Old Milwaukee!" repeats Becca.

"Old Milwaukee," I say, nodding stupidly.

And Julian winks at me.

"Hey—hey!" says Julian, "want to see something?"

We streak down Sixth Avenue, past rows of netted, bundled Christmas trees, Salvation Army Santas, holiday wanderers. We wind our way to Soho, Prince Street, restaurants, shops, galleries. Julian whirls along, pointing out sights and sounds. Finally, he stops at a small, closed gallery with several tiny pictures in the window. The girls look at the window—it's nice but seems no better or worse than any other shop. But Julian, grinning his Cheshire grin, points down, and there it is in the lower, right-hand corner of the window: a framed, paper-and-ink drawing of a snake-enwrapped fertility goddess. The picture is tiny, but the detail—the line work—is remarkable. The curves, the texture, the clarity. It's the smallest picture in the window, yet in fierce intensity all the other pictures pale. The tag on the picture says:

RAPTURE. $5,000. JULIAN GOLD.

"That's—that's incredible, Julian," I say. "It's beautiful."

"It's—good?" Lisette asks.

"It's him," I say, gesturing to Julian.

They look at him, confused.

"Him. *He's* Julian." I point to Julian, and I mime drawing—and then the drawing going into the window. And Julian grins idiotically, as the clouds lift from their eyes.

"You—make?" says Becca.

"And I have more inside," he says, pointing. "More inside!"

They look back and forth from the window to him. Becca presses her face to the glass, peering into the darkness to find more pictures. Finally, they comprehend their accomplishment: they've found an American Rock Star.

"We—come again—tomorrow!" says Julian. "See more!"

They nod, eagerly.

"Well, we will, anyway," he whispers to me.

Half an hour later, back at the apartment. An exhausted Becca sits sidled up to me on the couch, cradling a new beer, exploring a stack of Julian's drawings. I check my cell to see if Terri's called yet. Sounds of Julian and Lisette having loud sex emanate from my bedroom. Occasionally, Becca glances at me, sadly, left out. *What's wrong with you?* her eyes seem to say. *Why are we out here? Where's your art?*

I want to leave, but don't. I can't. I have absolutely nothing worthwhile going on in my life. Terri won't return my calls. I can barely finish a script, let alone sell one. I have no money, can barely pay rent. And when I do work, I'm temping at some pathetic law office or bank where I'm just filling space while someone else is on maternity leave.

Why can't I accept this gift? Why can't I accept this homely, but probably-not-so-bad Utrectian girl not quite wrapped up in a bow on my couch waiting for me to do something? Why can't I simply share the holiday with her? Why can't I let go?

The bedroom door opens a crack. And Julian pokes his head out and looks at me.

"No?" he says.

"No," I say.

"You sure?"

The sound of Lisette's voice comes from the room.

"Becca!"

Without a backwards glance, Becca jumps up, disappears into the bedroom, and closes the door.

As I mentioned, this notebook that I now hover above the water—this journal of my previous year—there's a lot of stuff in it. Meeting Terri for the first time—falling in love—perpetual fighting, breaking up, getting back together, over and over. I describe other women, too, and why I'm so useless around them. I review multiple lousy jobs—getting them, losing them—and why everything seems so meaningless and mundane all the time.

And there are other things: uninterpreted dreams; news of scripts sent out and rejected; restaurants eaten at; daily infractions and personal slights; money troubles; books read; movies seen; rarely acted upon ways to actually improve my condition; and some super rare moments of true joy and happiness.

There are non-diary-type things: bits; prompts; lists; two ideas that actually flower into something bigger (one being my current screenplay); and many, many fragments, most unlikely to have resonance or bear fruit for years to come.

When I drop it in, the pages—lovingly fanned as they are—will quickly soak up the bathwater like a thick, three-sectioned spiral-bound sponge. Words, thoughts, dialogue will melt into mush, junk, and a mist of blue ink will seep slowly, steadily into the water like that first swirl of unstirred Kool Aid. Then I'll push it deeper, deeper, watching it soak, watching ideas I may never exactly remember melt and die in front of me. I'll feel a sense of tightening, and then—then—that expected light-headedness, that release, that *What have I done? What have I done?! Fragments of scripts and ideas, elation, meeting Terri, no, no! What have I done?*

I wake, disoriented, on the couch around 2 a.m. Julian is there, reading intently.

"Where're the girls?" I ask.

"Other room," he says. "Asleep."

Great. I close my eyes.

"This is good stuff, Seth," says Julian. "Very therapeutic, I bet."

I blink my eyes open and see he's reading my journal.

"Hey. Hey," I say. "Jesus Christ, Julian."

"I very much like the pages with the giant words. Have you considered burning it?"

"What?"

"You should. You should make a bonfire. Right here. This. Everything. Throw it all in."

"Shut up."

"It's tying you down, man. Closing you off."

He shows me the pages with the big words.

"This is the equivalent of screaming, yes?"

"Julian—"

"I mean—why not just scream? It's so much easier."

And he screams, at the top of his lungs. And God, I've got a headache. He screams again, grinning, jumping about the room.

"Julian—someone's gonna call 911—"

Lisette comes to the door in T-shirt and underwear, groggy, reacting to the noise.

"Uh?" she says.

"Look at this," says Julian, throwing her my notebook. She looks at it, sees giant meaningless words.

"Destroy it, man. Burn it. It's the only way! Want me to?"

"No."

"Happy to do it. Happy to help."

Now, Becca is up, too.

"Hullo," says Becca, yawning. She plops down near me on the couch, rubs up against me like a tired cat, lays her head in my lap. She sees the pile of Julian's sketches on the floor, picks through them. Lisette goes through my fridge, finds a pint of ice cream.

"You think it's crazy. It's not," says Julian.

He reaches down and takes the pile of sketches and fans them out to Becca.

"Pick one," he says.

Her eyes light up, flattered. She chooses a delicate but breathtakingly detailed drawing of some Hindu-like elephant God surrounded by arrows and stars.

"Good choice," he says. "No copy."

And he rips it in half.

"No!" says Becca, reaching for the picture—but he pushes her hands away.

"Don't touch," he says, ripping it in half again and again until it's in little pieces. Lisette, befuddled, eats ice cream.

"See how easy that was?! And that picture was extremely important to me. But I owe it nothing. It has no hold on me, man."

He chooses another and tears it up, too. He offers the stack to me.

"Go on. Pick one!"

"They're yours to rip," I say. "I couldn't care less."

"I'm not ripping them. I'm setting myself free."

"*You're* free?"

"Absolutely."

I stare at him.

"Can we call it a day, please?"

"Actually," he grins, "no. Time for Round Two."

"Round Two?"

"Absolutely," he says, turning to Lisette and Becca. "And I am so sick of these girls. Aren't you sick of these girls?"

Becca, tired, confused, kneels on the floor trying to piece the elephant picture back together. Lisette kneels beside her, tries to help. Julian puts his hands on their backs.

"Time to go, girls," he says. "Party's over."

They stare at him, confused. He jumps up, grinning, as full of energy as he was six or seven hours ago. He goes into the bedroom, brings out their clothes—socks, jeans, shoes—and throws them at the girls.

"Party's over!" he repeats, opening the front door. "Time to go! Time to fucking get out and let us get on with our lives!"

Becca looks at Lisette, frightened. They murmur to each other in Utrechtian or Norwegian or I have no idea what. They're beginning to understand and feel a bit used, tired, pissed. *Who the fuck is this guy? Oh no. No, no. It's late. We're not going anywhere.*

Now they're looking at me for help.

"You stay out of it," Julian snaps at me.

He reaches down and aggressively lifts Becca up, lifts Lisette up. But they push back, pull his hands off them. He shoves their clothes at them.

"The party is fucking over!" he shouts. "Now! Get the fuck out!"

"Julian—" I say.

"No!" he turns on me, yelling like a Master telling his dog to sit.

Finally, the girls are getting their pants on, sweaters. They're cursing at him in Teutonic gibberish.

"Get out! Get out! Get out!" he says.

He looks at me.

"They don't get it," he says.

He collects their shoes, coats, and goes to the window facing the back alley. He opens it.

"Out," he says, throwing their coats out the window.

"No!" yell the girls, freaked out. They jump up, scratching him, grabbing for their shoes, trying to halt him.

"No!" they yell while Julian laughs, dangling shoes out the window.

"Get—out!" he says, flinging their shoes out the window. And I can hear them clanking against garbage cans in the back alley.

"Just—go," he says, calmly.

They grab their bags and purses and move quickly. Becca, mustering up some nerve, grabs some of his pictures and flings them out the window. Lisette smacks him, and they hurry to the door, cursing him—and then cursing me for being less than useless.

And Julian hurries over and shuts and locks the door. He goes back to the window and watches a moment later as they collect their things in the alley below.

"This is too funny," says Julian. "C'mere. You gotta see this!"

I hear them outside cursing him more. A moment passes. The voices dim. He starts to close the window, then stops. Instead, he picks up my notebook.

"Want me to throw?" he asks.

"No," I say.

"You need to throw it out the window. You need me to do this."

"Put it down, Julian. It's not yours to throw."

"Pussy," he says, putting it down. "Don't forget that. You're shackled to this. By your own choice. This is a cage of your making."

"Mm."

"Okay!" he says, pulling a small energy drink out of his backpack and downing it. "Round Two! Let's go!"

"It's the middle of the night."

"Come on. Fifty dollars says I get three more by noon tomorrow!"

"Go by yourself."

"Stop saying *no!* Just stop it, Seth! All your life—*no, no, no.* You're fucking miserable! You're like death, here. This is a fucking coffin in the middle of New York!"

"Uh-huh."

"I'll go without you."

"Please do."

"I will."

"Good. Go."

"Give me a key."

I point to the junk drawer next to the stove. He opens it and finds and pockets the key.

"Please come with me," he says. "Please."

"No," I say. "Go to sleep and we'll go in the morning."

"Douche," he says.

"Three girls by noon," he says.

And he's gone.

It's a bit after 9 a.m. when I wake. The room is bright, but hazy and very cold. The door to my bedroom is open. I appear to be alone. Julian has found three girls and gone God knows where and I don't care. If I never see him again, fine.

Why didn't I help those girls? Because I was tired? Disoriented? For the same reason I didn't have sex with either of them? Fear? Fear that something—anything— would go wrong. Some odd something? Some intangible, irrational thing—that I would regret if not now, then eventually. So, instead, I do nothing. Nothing. Trapped in my own living tomb.

I realize, he's right. He's right. I have to stop this. I have to let go.

I have to kill the notebook.

But I can't rip it up, or throw it out the window, or set a goddamn fire in my tiny, shithole apartment. What ritual can I enact that will permanently exorcise this demon? And then it becomes obvious.

So, I stand above my bathtub, fanning out pages. I'm not afraid. I can do this. Remove the chains. I can. I can. I can.

But I don't.

Oh no.

Of course not. Not even the slightest bit. Not to this poor, harmless thing—with stories of my life and loves and ideas and fragments. I value these scribblings—that have no meaning to anyone but me—more than anything I own, more than most relationships I get into. For me, drowning this worn, lifeless, spiral thing—this inanimate object—would be akin to drowning a puppy.

Why is it so goddamn cold?

I put the notebook down and drain the tub. I come back into the living room and see the window is still open from the previous night. I go to shut it, but poke my head out, curious to see if there's any clothes or pictures still down there. But when I look down what I see are legs. Scrawny legs, in ripped jeans, akimbo in the snow. Someone is lying down there—and then—the legs move. Someone's lying on the ground down there—and then I see—a long, red tassel.

Julian.

Two days later, Julian's mother arrives from Milwaukee to bring him home from the hospital. By the time she arrives she's heard the story several times—that he was mugged returning to my building—and now she just wants to get him out of New York.

The "mugging" leaves Julian a bit of a mess. He had been hit from behind with a blunt object, a tire iron, or a shovel. His glasses were shattered. He cracked a couple teeth. The mugger—muggers?—repeatedly kicked him in the stomach, leaving him with a fractured rib and internal bleeding. His wallet was gone, and also, oddly, were his shoes. The police considered this a particularly extreme assault, as Julian was not simply beaten and robbed, but the assailant(s) appear to have defecated on him, as well. The police asked me if there might have been anything personal about the crime. I told them that I had been asleep. However, in the nine years I'd lived in the building, above junkies and crack victims and the like, I'd never personally run into trouble. Maybe, they considered, it was because of how colorfully he was dressed.

I see Julian for just a few moments as his mother wheels him out to the cab. In a slurred, drugged voice he whispers to me, "nailed one in the bathroom at McSorley's."

The next day it snows again. I'm still a temp, still without money, still stuck in the worst apartment in New York. But somehow, I don't feel quite so miserable anymore. In fact, I feel pretty good. And I decide I ought to do something with that.

So, I sit that night in a crowded East Village bar and get good and drunk and stare at this young woman with short, red hair for a couple hours. I have intense, chaotic plans of things we can do. Finally, I make my way over to her. But before I can speak, she says *creep!* and leaves with her friends.

I still feel good though, and I make another, better plan. The bar I realize—the bar and the girl and Julian and Lisette and Becca—they've all been a test. A test of my love for Terri, which I now realize is terribly, terribly real. Now I have clarity. I'll go home and sleep off this drunk, and then call on Terri tomorrow.

Returning home, my conviction grows stronger. I feel alive and free and hopeful and good, and I do what I always do when I feel alive and free and hopeful and good, which is to write it all down in my journal.

Tomorrow, I write, *I will go to a Korean deli and get the best bouquet of flowers and go over to Terri's. Maybe it will be a futile effort. Maybe not. I don't care. I will say to her all the things I ever meant to say, but had fearfully written down instead: that I do love her; that she ought to be treated better; that she ought to be worshipped.*

I write all of this in big, gigantic letters, and then trace over and over them—to emphasize seriousness, hope, and conviction.

I WILL MAKE THIS WORK, I write.

THINGS WILL BE GOOD, I write.

TOMORROW.

The #$@!# Bicycle Boys!—Adventure #46:

The #$@!# Bicycle Boys Save Christmas, Again!

"*S*ANTA CLAUS HAS BEEN #$@!# KIDNAPPED!*" EXCLAIMED the President of the United States.

"Christ!" said Flip. "Again? He was just kidnapped last year!"

"I'm afraid so," said the President. His image, replete with panic sweat, on the HD Etherlogic Hollerphone made the situation all the more urgent.

"The #$!@ FBI and military are baffled," he continued. "And frankly, time is running out! This is a crisis only The #$@!# Bicycle Boys can handle!"

"Understood, sir," I said.

"I'm forwarding all the information we've got, boys. But it's slim."

"Not a problem, sir."

"Thanks. Gotta run!"

It had been a long, stressful year and we were pretty $#%!@ tired. Flip and I had just gotten back from our annual Thanksgiving adventure—*The Case of the Punk @$$ Pilgrim*—and before we could even sit down, our latest case had started.

"Seems like we never get a $%&*# break," said Flip. He printed out the reports from the #$!@ FBI.

"You're just stressed," I said. "Our last adventure was pretty exhausting."

"And we just got back from that one! Boy—for five minutes I'd just like to have *The Adventure of the *%&$# Kids Who Parked Themselves in Front of the $#%!@ Tube and Ate #$@!# Pizza!*"

"Yes, and it doesn't help that we have to walk everywhere. We really should fix our bikes."

"Our $%&!@ bikes!"

"Yes," I said.

Our bikes had gotten flat tires three adventures ago and we'd been so distracted that we hadn't had time to fix them. Of course, this actually made the titles of our exploits misnomers since Flip and Chip, the celebrated #$@!# Bicycle Boys (Junior Detectives) no longer had rideable bikes.

It also didn't help that we had grown a backlog of unsolved cases, especially *The Quandary of the Missing %$@#& Cash*. Recently, almost 90 percent of the world's cash had completely disappeared. Some suspected it had been funneled down a massive hole to the Underworld. But we hadn't had time to investigate with the holiday-related crimes keeping us so busy.

"We really should look into the missing %$@#& cash when we get a chance," I said to Flip.

"Yeah, whatever," said Flip, sifting through the President's download. "This data is complete horse #!@&#!"

"Well, it *is* from the government," I said.

"Yeah. We better find Bixby."

Bixby the Boy Genius lived in the house next door to us. Bixby was the sweet, innocent five-year-old who supplied us with all our high-tech gadgetry. His lab was fully $%★&# loaded.

"What concerns me," said Bixby, in a quiet, unassuming voice, "is all this stress. The world's stress levels are unprecedented this year—"

"Tell us a-$%#!#-bout it!" said Flip. "We started the year on Adventure #9—and we're already on Adventure #46, for $%#@ sake! Y'know how far behind we are on our regular $@#& schoolwork?! Forget about it!"

"Would you like me to whip up a device to do it for you?"

"Sure," said Flip.

"No, no," I said. "Thanks, anyway. Listen, Bixby—"

"I've been doing stress experiments here in the vault," said Bixby. "It's very interesting. If you'd like to—"

"We really have to focus on Santa, Bixby. We'd be happy to look at your stress vault later."

"Yeah, in our next $%$#@ adventure," said Flip.

"*Flip!*" I said.

"Yeah, sorry, whatever."

Typically, in our adventures, Flip was the headstrong, aggressive one, while I remained thoughtful and agreeable. Although I certainly had my moments.

"I'm running the feed on Santa now," said Bixby. "The list of possible suspects is wide: Pink Freud, Cyclopatra, The Crooked Man—"

"Ricky the Rogue Elf, Count Oobleck, The ReGifter," added Flip.

"The Gwim Weeper, The Bird Flipper," I contributed.

"Tommy Chugalug, Joan of Noah's Ark," piped in Bixby.

"A is for Arsonist, The Outgoing President," gargled Flip.

"Rhoda the Exploda," interrupted Bixby. "Jack B. Quiche—"

"Mm—he only committed quiche-related crimes," I clarified.

"Right," said Bixby.

"It could've been The Splintererer," I suggested.

"The Splintererer?" said Flip. "Was it the Splintererer or the Splinterererer?"

"The Splinterererer was the grandnephew of the original Splintererer. He added the extra 'er' to differentiate himself."

"Look," said Flip. "It's gotta be Count Oobleck, right? I mean—it was him last $%$#@ year!"

"Yes, that would make sense," I said.

"$%!@& sense," Flip corrected me.

"Yes," I said.

"According to this," said Bixby, reading off his monitor screen, "Count Oobleck is still locked away at Atticazkabananaramastan."

"Not to mention Oobleck hates to repeat himself," I said.

"According to this," said Bixby, "Santa was last seen at the North Pole two days ago. Looks like you're headed there, boys."

"*Oh crap!*" said Flip. "Crap crap crap crap crap! I $%!@$ hate the $%!@$ North Pole! It's $%!@$ freezing!"

"Flip's pretty stressed out, Bixby," I said.

"I can see that," said Bixby, yawning. Bixby still took naps during the day and hadn't had one in hours. "Maybe my stress experiment could—"

"*Not now!*" said Flip.

"Would it help if I fixed your bikes?"

"If you have something that could keep us warm at the Pole," I said. "That would be terrific."

Getting to the North Pole was the easy part. After forty-six adventures Flip and I had quite a number of options. There was The Mystical Basement, The Dream Sewer, The Fantabulous Tool Shed, The Nexus of All Realities Construction Site, The Hyperbolic Port-a-San, The Infinite Drainage Ditch, The Interspacial Doghouse, The Improbable Empty Refrigerator Box, The Overflowing Time Puddle, The Next-Door Neighbor's Closed-for-the-Winter Pool Paradox, The Physics-Ignoring Pup Tent, The Completely Irrational Large Recycling Container, The Miraculous

Moped (with sidecar), and of course, The Remarkable Abandoned Minivan.

Of course, quite a few had broken down or were one-shot deals. The Mystical Basement and Improbable Empty Refrigerator Box couldn't be used more than once, The Overflowing Time Puddle only worked during heavy rains, and The Interspacial Doghouse had collapsed in a fit of poorly constructed obsolescence.

But the Remarkable Abandoned Minivan—or RAM for short—worked just fine. Unfortunately, we had left the Minivan in an athletic field, three miles away, after our Thanksgiving adventure. Of course, our bikes still had flats. So, we started walking, Flip complaining all the way.

When we arrived at the North Pole, Mrs. Claus was distraught . . . and squinting quite a bit.

"He finished his last shift and went to bed," said Mrs. Claus. "And in the morning, he was gone!"

"And no sign that he'd grabbed a @!#&% sled and went off on his own?" asked Flip.

"*Flip!*" I said.

"Well, maybe he was stressed, too?" said Flip.

"There was nothing," said Mrs. Claus.

"What about Ricky?" I asked.

"Oooh, I don't like to think of him at all," said Mrs. Claus, squinting nervously.

I pressed a button on my two-way watch. Bixby sent a quick response.

"Hmm," I said. "Bixby says Ricky's still in *BED*."

BED—the Bad Elf Detention center—was the North Pole's reformatory for delinquent elves. Not too many people even knew the North Pole had a reformatory. But some of the elves were exceedingly naughty.

"Maybe we should pay Ricky a little @!#&% visit," said Flip.

"Would you like the elves to build you new bikes, boys?" asked Mrs. Claus.

"No time," said Flip. "Maybe on the #$!@ rebound!"

"Thanks, anyway," I said. "By the way, is something wrong with your vision?"

"Oh, it's my @!#&%—*oh, excuse me!*" she said, blushing. "It's my spectacles. I've misplaced them again. I hate them but can't live without them!"

"Well, when we're done with the next few adventures, we'll add that to the #$!@ pile," said Flip.

And with that we were off.

BED was on the dark side of Kringle Mountain. The detention center didn't have a huge population, but the inmates weren't the kind you'd want to find yourself next to in a dark chimney.

Ricky, especially, was a nasty piece of work with razor sharp ears and a long snaggletooth. Though seeing him in his cell, I noticed that his long, gnarled tooth was actually gone. Perhaps BED had acquired some decent dentists.

"If it isn't The #$@!# Bicycle Boys!" snarled Ricky, in a cute, yet belligerent squeal. "Well, whatever y'want—I don't know nothin'!"

"You knew a lot last #$%@ year when you helped Count Oobleck snare Santa!" said Flip.

"That was last $#@!@ year and this is this $#@!@ year, smart guy!" said Ricky.

Ricky seemed particularly stressed.

"If I remember correctly," said Flip, "you used to be pretty $!##@ proud of your work, Ricky."

"What's it to ya?" said Ricky.

Flip held up a Historical Dames doll—a popular toy that Ricky had worked on before he'd gone rogue. Flip bent the doll's right arm backwards.

"Hey! Hey! Don't do that!" cried Ricky, agitated.

I hated when Flip did things like this. But some villains required tougher actions.

"Was it Oobleck? Tommy Chugalug? The Crooked Man?" barked Flip.

"If I tell ya," whined Ricky, "this place won't be safe for me no more!"

Flip grabbed Ricky through the bars.

"*Safe!* My bike's got two flat tires! Y'think that's safe?"

"Flip!" I yelled. "Enough!"

I pulled Flip off Ricky. The good boy detective/bad boy detective routine wasn't working.

"If we get Santa back," I said, "we'll see what we can do."

"I heard," said Ricky, "that The Crooked Man was up to something. Didn't think he ever got 'round to it, though."

Flip and I looked at each other and headed out.

"Hey! Hey!" called Ricky. "What about me?!"

Flip tossed the doll into the cell.

"Baby!" said Ricky.

Flip and I made our way to the minivan while Bixby shot me The Crooked Man's coordinates.

"#$@!# elf," Flip grumbled.

"Flip," I said, "look—how about if we take a break from all the cursing for a couple hours?"

"A couple #$@!# hours?!"

"An hour and a half? One hour!"

"Fine—alright. I'll take one for the #@—for the team."

"Thanks," I said. "I appreciate it."

I plugged Bixby's coordinates into the van's console, while Flip surveyed our gadgetry. A second later the van *BLIPPED* out of, and then back into, existence—right outside The Crooked Man's lair.

The Crooked Man, as you can imagine, had a particularly frightening hideout. A crooked house at the edge of a crooked cliff amidst gloomy, crooked mountains. Even the sky itself—

"Yeah, yeah, we get it," said Flip. "Can I start cursing again?"

"No," I said.

But as we exited the minivan, we were both dumbstruck. We were on a lush mountain road leading up to an ordinary, white picket fence house. The trees looked like trees. The sky like sky.

"Nothing's crooked," said Flip.

"Hmm, I said. "Maybe The Crooked Man went straight?"

"Ba dump bump," said Flip. "Don't forget to tip your waitress."

We snuck up to the house, our 390 Magnum Auto Vapor Nets at the ready.

"Better to go around back," said Flip.

"Agreed," I said.

What we found behind the house was startling: a beautiful garden with a normal, little old man pulling weeds. We crept over, quietly. Malevolently, the man sprang on us.

"*The #$@!# Bicycle Boys!?* Whadda you want?!"

"Who the $#%!@ are you?" asked Flip.

"Flip!"

"What?! It's been an hour!"

"Not even!"

"I'm The $#!@& Crooked Man!" said The Crooked Man. "Who d'ya think?!"

"You're not crooked," said Flip.

"I was. Every inch of me was crooked until last night! There I was—sitting by my crooked fireplace with my crooked cat and crooked—"

"Yeah, yeah! We got it!" said Flip.

"Planning the *perfect* way to ruin Christmas! But when I awoke this morning everything was $#!@& straight! Look at this!"

He held up the most beautiful, perfect cat. It mewed.

"Nice," I said.

"Bah!" said The Crooked Man, flinging it away. "Now look at me—reduced to planting weeds!"

"Planting?" said Flip.

"You did this! You!" he shouted, holding up the gardening spade, threateningly. "Give me back my crooks!"

"We don't have 'em, y'goat!" said Flip.

The old man began flinging topsoil at us.

"C'mon," I said to Flip. We headed back to the van amid a hail of dirt.

"Well, now what?" said Flip. "We've got no clues. The whole thing's a bust!"

"Oh no," I said. "We've got plenty of clues. Think about it. Santa disappeared. The Crooked Man's crooks disappeared. What else?"

"My free time?"

"No, really—"

Flip thought about it.

"The cash."

"Ninety percent of all the world's cash."

"Think it's related?"

"Bixby," I spoke into my watch. "I'm sending you data. See, if you can—Bixby?"

"What?"

"He's not responding—"

I went to the van's console and plugged in the information. A minute later, a set of numbers appeared. My eyes lit up, stunned.

"What is it?"

I looked at Flip, gravely.

"We need to get back."

By the time the minivan returned to our block, a throbbing, interspacial vortex had enveloped Bixby's house and was consuming everything in its path.

"This is his $%!#@ Stress Experiment!?" Flip yelled over 120-mile-per-hour winds.

"We've got to get in there!" I shouted.

We fired our 490 GPG Turbine Vortex Disrupters at the tempest but they ricocheted off.

"We'll have to use the van!" I yelled.

"To get inside the vortex?!"

"Yes! Into the lab!"

"That's $%#!@ crazy!"

"It's our only chance—and technically, we did something very similar in Adventure #—"

"Yeah, yeah, whatever—just do it!"

Dodging debris, we climbed into the minivan and set the controls for inside the lab. The van rocked violently, buckling inward from the pressure.

"It's collapsing!" called Flip.

"She'll hold!" I yelled.

And she did. A moment later the crushed minivan had *BLIPPED* itself inside Bixby's lab. Bixby was there, unconscious on the floor. Nearby, the heart of what had been his experimental vault pulsed and writhed. We roused Bixby to his feet.

"Bixby! Can you shut it off?!"

"I tried to stabilize it, but it's absorbed too much!"

Inside the vault a miniature universe thrashed and wriggled.

"What is that thing, anyway?" Flip yelled.

"Well, my Mum and Dad were always arguing about money—in fact, I realized everyone was always arguing about money—"

"So, you built a device to suck it all up?!" said Flip.

"To reduce things to their component atoms," said Bixby, "and then suck it all up, yes."

"Everything that causes stress?" I yelled.

"Basically," said Bixby.

"Bixby!" yelled Flip, angrily. "Removing all the stuff that causes $%#!@ stress causes *even more* $%#!@ stress! Now, there's nothing *but* $%#!@ stress!"

"*Would you please stop cursing?*" I yelled at Flip. *"It's not helping!"*

"I've tried to put things back," called Bixby, "but I can't do it fast enough! I've already put back all the credit reports and military weapons and personal digital devices and that's when I got hit by the feedback!"

"Did you put the cash back?" I asked.

"Not yet—"

"Put that back now, Bixby!"

Bixby pressed a button and the vault heaved. Suddenly, it was smaller but still pulsing.

"Alright!" said Bixby. "I've redistributed the wealth!"

"Oh $%!@# perfect," said Flip.

"But it still won't shut down!"

I went over to the crumpled van.

"We'll use the minivan's engine to move the vault—"

"Where?" said Flip.

"Where it can't hurt anybody!" I said. *"Into the sun!"*

"Well, that's pretty $%#!@ contrived!" yelled Flip.

"Sorry!" I yelled back. "No time to be more $%#!@ creative!"

"What about the people still in there?" said Flip.

"The engine should just move the vault," said Bixby. "Everything else will stay here! But we'll have to restabilize as much as possible, first! I think I've gotten most of the elected officials out!"

"I've set the controls on the minivan!" I yelled. "Brace yourselves!"

"I $%!@# hate this!" shouted Flip.

Bixby and I hit our buttons. There was an earth-shattering *BELCH!*

And then everything went black.

I awoke soon after lying in the street, a block away from Bixby's. His house was gone, and the vault's explosion had spewed hundreds of reintegrated people and objects in a wide radius: cars, boats, swimming pools, telemarketers, bank employees, airline and travel representatives, offshore technology companies, mortgage brokers, dieting manuals, tons upon tons of jewelry, gold, silver, oil, and dozens upon dozens of celebrities. (Later, we also discovered Ricky's snaggletooth, numerous crooked artifacts, and Mrs. Claus's spectacles.)

Nearby, Bixby and Flip were bruised but recovering.

And wandering down the street, in an absolute daze, was Santa Claus.

Within an hour, Flip, Bixby, and I had escorted Santa back to the North Pole via The Hyperbolic Port-a-San (which no one was particularly keen on using). Mrs. Claus and the elves were elated to have Santa back and she served us hot cocoa in his office.

"But why did the vault suck *me* up?" asked Santa.

"Are you kidding?" said Flip. "No offense, Santa—you're a good guy and all, but talk about stress!"

"I suppose the holidays can be a bit—uhm—well—"

"*A bit?!*" said Flip.

"Nick," interrupted Mrs. Claus, "as long as the boys are here, why don't you give them their presents?" She elbowed him in the ribs, knowingly, and left the office.

"Yes, well, that sounds alright," said Santa. "Why not?"

He went over to a massive, ornate book on a back table, and began flipping through pages. He rested his hot cocoa on the shelf above and lost himself in reading. Flip and I exchanged bored looks.

"Really, Santa," I said. "It's not necessary—"

"Mm . . . let's see," said Santa. "We've put in an order to build Bixby a new house. That should be easy enough—"

"Thank you, Santa," said Bixby.

Santa kept reading. Then he chuckled, surprised.

"Oh ho!" he said. "I hadn't expected this! It seems Flip and Chip have been cursing up a storm this year!"

"So?" said Flip.

"So, I've got both of you on the naughty list! I'm afraid I don't have *anything* for you boys this year!"

"We just saved the $#@#& world!" said Flip. "Not to mention your sorry—"

"Flip!" I said.

"Well," said Santa, "That's no excuse for a potty mouth. You'll just have to do better next year! Ho ho ho!"

"*Next year?!*" said Flip. "You want us to try harder *next year?*"

"Ho ho ho! Perhaps, if you added a few more adventures—"

But before Santa could finish that thought, he accidentally bumped the shelf above him, dislodging his steaming hot cocoa, and spilling it all over his back. He began jumping and screaming, maniacally.

"YOW!" said Santa, surprising us all. "YOW! YOW! YOW! OH $%#@! HOLY #$%!@! WHO PUT THAT $%&!@ UP THERE #$%!@ WHAT ARE YOU #$%!@ NUTS?! TRYING TO $%&!@# KILL ME!? $%!#@ THAT $%&★!@ IS #$%!@ HOT! #$%!@#$%!@ #$%!@ #$%!@ $%&!@# $%&★!@ $%@!#$%@! @#$★&#&$@! #&$%#!@ @#$$$@!! #%$@!@#@##%!"

"Santa—?"

But Santa was running around the room, flailing his arms and shouting every curse he could think of. Flip, Bixby, and I watched, flabbergasted.

"Talk about stress," said Flip.

"#$%!@ #$%!@ Son of a—$%&★!@" said Santa, still flailing.

Flip grabbed the nearby pitcher of water and threw it on Santa. Soaked, but calmer, he collapsed backwards into his office chair.

"Hoo boy!!" he said. "Thanks!"

He leaned forward, catching his breath, and nursing his wounded back.

"Wow! Ooochie!"

Finally, he looked up, realizing we were still there. His face turned as red as his coat.

"Oh! Yes. Well. Uhm, right. Flip and Chip—Bicycle Boys—here we are!" He looked back at his book and quickly rubber-stamped Nice! over our names.

"Must've been a misprint!" he muttered, and gingerly ushered us to the door.

"There you go. Thanks, again! Merry Christmas! See Elf 287 on your way out—"

Flip, Bixby, and I headed through the toy factory back to the Port-a-San.

"Y'know, Flip," I said. "If you think about it this adventure really didn't have any villains."

"Oh, please," said Flip. "Kidnapping's a felony for $$%#! sake! Bixby totally got lucky!"

"Well, anyway," I said, "I think the best part was when you stopped cursing for almost an hour. What a relief! I myself stopped cursing quite early on, in case you hadn't noticed—"

"I noticed," said Flip. "You should go back to cursing."

Waiting for us by the Port-a-San was Elf 287 with a large, shiny box.

"Here y'go, boys!" he said, eagerly.

Flip opened it and inside was a beautiful, silver bicycle repair kit, and a pump.

"#$%!@ this!" said Flip, shoving it back at the elf.

"Agreed," I said.

"You bet," said Bixby.

And we all went home.

Mrs. Harris

Hello? Mrs. Harris? Mrs. Harris? It's Noel Robbins again. Are you there? Hello? Happy holidays, I guess. Okay. Okay. I'm trying to be polite and civil and responsible, here, but I've sort-of had it with this. As you know—and as I've mentioned in these calls several times— we appear to have very similar phone numbers; like just a digit off or something. So, look, again you've given out my phone number instead of yours to all of your clients or case files or whatever you call them. This has been going on now for several weeks. And while it's been extremely annoying to me and my family—your clients are now also very upset.

I've taken some notes. This is just a small sampling. You might want to get a pen. Mr. Lee hasn't received any welfare checks for the past two weeks and is running out of food. And it's Christmastime. Miss Osorio needs your permission to sign up for a particular methadone clinic. She's very concerned. "Concerned" is the wrong word—"panicky, freaked out, and possibly self-destructive" may be more appropriate. But we can leave it at "concerned." She's concerned, and it's Christmas. Ms. Guzman is paranoid that her old boyfriend is following her and wants to hurt her. She doesn't know what to do. I suggested she call 911 but she seemed to think that you and I work together and wanted me to, I don't know, come get her. Which is my fault, really. Honestly, why I suggested anything I have no idea, except that I just—I don't know—I *felt* for her. Y'know? I mean I feel for all these people. How could you not at this time of year? But that's beside the point.

What else? Mr. Solano wants to know if you're looking into his housing situation. He calls a lot. He'd like to have a stable, settled place for the holidays. Mr. Davis—Mr. Davis—just wants someone to talk to. Anyone. He's just—*alone*. And I have been talking to him. I've talked to him a couple times, already. He seems very nice. But I'm not—I'm not a professional, Mrs. Harris. I'm out of my league, here.

And there are others. This list goes on and on and on.

Mrs. Harris, you *must* give these people the right number. *You must.* I can't imagine it will take you more than five minutes to—to fix whatever this sheet is that you're sending out to them.

Let me reiterate—I am not changing my number. I've had my number for over fourteen years now. This is *my* number. I have no idea what your circumstances are, and I've tried to steer these people to your office. But they don't understand what I'm saying. They want me to help them. I can't help them. I wish I could. But I can't. I'm an associate graphic designer. And I'm probably going to take a pay cut at the end of this year in this shitty economy. Which really pisses me off, but—but—that's not the point, anyway. Right? The point is these calls are not my calls. They're upsetting me and they're upsetting my family.

Mrs. Harris, I spoke to your office and they said whatever sheet you're sending out is locked and they can't change it. They say *you* have to unlock and change it. So, I am asking you, please, please, for the last time, please, do the right thing and fix this worksheet.

And—and one more thing, Mrs. Harris. I didn't want it to come to this, but well—your office did one thing for me. They gave me your home phone number. So, look, if you can't contact me and confirm that you've changed this number by this weekend—I'm—I'm going to leave a message on my answering machine instructing these people to call you—at your home phone number. I'm sorry,

Mrs. Harris, but honestly, you leave me no choice. So, again, if I don't—*hello? Mrs. Harris?*

Oh, you are there?

Oh. Yes. Well. Yes.

Yes. Happy holidays to you, too.

Hello.

Telethon

WELCOME BACK TO THE *PBS CHANNEL 18 HOLIDAY Pledge Drive*. I'm Clark Sims. For those of you now joining us, we've just seen the first four minutes of *Citizen Kane*—possibly the greatest film in cinema history —and we'll continue to watch this extraordinary film in regularly interrupted, four-minute intervals over the next twenty-four hours.

But first, we'd like to remind you that it's you—*You!*, the *Channel 18* subscriber—that makes all of our great programming possible.

Programs like *Travels with Wingo, Bill Moyers Underwater, Thursday Night Whale Film, Death of an Ant, Hop For Life, Samovar!, You Be the Mime, Big Caesar Salad, Dog Day Fix-It-Up, Oh Peg!, Walk With Cancer, Kelp Discovery, This Old Shithouse, Falafel Town Meeting*, and of course, our premier show *Our Delusionally Happy Servants*.

You'll also enjoy our English comedies: *Desperate Turk, Fish & Chips, I'm the Queen, Escher Rehash, Bungalow*

Journey, Barber & Barber, Cornflakes!, Spoof Now, That's My Telly, and *Call Inspector Nancy!*

And don't forget our world-renowned children's programming with shows like *Treacle Factory, Teeter Totter, Unctuous Caleb, Chewy Chewy Chewy, Wish Fulfillment, Penis Gallery, Mop Stuff!, WHAT WHAT?,* and *Secret Sweatshop*—now in its sixty-fourth season!

That's right. Our programming is mainlined straight to you—*You!*—our dear darling membership. You said, I don't want reality TV! Bring me *Fish & Chips* with Reginald Arno! And we listened. And that's what you've got.

I'm sorry? What's that? *Not a member?!* And yet, *you're watching?* That's not very fair. Coasting off actual paying members! I'll bet there's one with you right now! Staring at you! *Glaring!* Why—there she is! Right across the room! She looks quite angry! Well, sure! You're watching her programming *for free!*

Wait—hold on—is that a knife?! Whoa! Someone's territorial about PBS! Careful! She's coming at you—*Dodge! Dodge!* Alright—quickly—one thing to do! Whip out that checkbook—that's right—feign back—good! Okay! Now! While she's confused—backing off—quickly now! Make it *Payable to Channel 18.* That's it! Good! You've got her now! *Write $300!* Yes! Yes! Sign it! Mail it in! Ah!

She's dropped the knife! Sinking back into the recliner! *Whew!* Close one! See? There—she looks so relaxed now . . .

Probably because she only pledged $20.

And now let's return to the next four minutes of that extraordinary film . . .

Citizen Kane!

Grampa Lou's Legacy

I'M A HAPPIER PERSON NOW. CAN'T YOU TELL? I SAY THAT because I've been working at it steadily for almost a year now. I was not always this way. In fact, up until about three months ago, I was an empty, self-esteem-less, smoldering-pile-of-shit person, but then something just clicked and that was the end of it. No event. No trigger. One day, I just woke up and knew I could let go of the death of my marriage.

It's Christmas Eve and I've been "home" for a few days now. Mom's in the kitchen, cooking. Dad's gone to pick up Gramma Lou. Dottie, my little sister, and Mark, her husband, will be here in a couple of hours. Then everyone will be *home for the holidays.*

The house is abundantly Christmassy—stockings, wreaths, mistletoe hanging from everything, an over-ornamented tree. Mom's goal every year is to continually surpass herself with the tree. To add more and more—ornaments, lights, baubles, things—until barely an inch of green is visible. And of course, the fireplace crackles.

Since the divorce, everyone—particularly Dad—treats me like an invalid. And not in a fun way. Sunday night, he took me aside, confidentially, and actually suggested that I move back home, into my old room. At age forty.

"You could work at *any* school, Irmie. You have friends here. You'd have a support system."

"You mean a family?"

"Well . . . sure, you'd have that, too."

When I first arrived home earlier this week, I had strong urges to not leave the house. Leaving the house meant running into people—old friends, neighbors—all of whom would ask me about *the books*.

Seventeen years ago, at age twenty-three, I'd written and successfully gotten published two short books: an incredibly forgettable *Star Trek* novel, *Hephaestus' Fire* (ST263) (I was way into it in college), and a soulless but extremely popular "teen" novel, *Alanna Alone*, which would become the single thing most associated with me for the rest of my life.

At the mall:

"*Irma!* Oh my God! Look at you! Lori! Lori—this is Irma! Lori just read your book! Wow! Lori loved it!"

"Yeah. S'okay," says the disinterested thirteen-year-old daughter with glittering rainbow braces.

"I just read it again! And, y'know I didn't remember it being that good! See, Lori! I *said* I knew her!"

"You wrote a *Star Trek* book, too, right?"

"That's right."

"My brother read it. He said you got Spock wrong."

"Tell him I apologize. I wrote it a long time ago."

"*Two* books? *Who knew!* Did you ever write anything else?"

I skipped three high school reunions just to avoid the question *Did you ever write anything else?* And I did, by the way. I wrote some television, three plays, a couple of articles on oarfish. (Don't ask.) Now, I have a very full life teaching high school out west. In fact, I've actually done quite well for myself, thank you.

I should've used a pseudonym.

Dad's gone to pick up Gramma Lou. That's Louella. She's ninety-two years old. I specifically came home this year to spend time at her house, going through my Grampa Lou's (Louis) journals. I've been saying I was going to do this since the year after he died, when I was fifteen.

From what I understand, Grampa Lou and I would have gotten along. And supposedly we had a lot in common: dark, brown eyes; a sardonic, moody temperament; inappropriate guttural laughs; and, of course, we were both failed writers. Okay, yeah, I got two books published, whereas Grampa never published anything. Still, at this point, I figure we're just about even.

But my secret mission on this trip was to finally give Grampa his literary due. Dive deep deep into his papers. Explore. Excavate. Find something. Edit, possibly, if I felt the need to. (Or not.) I had three days and two heavy trunks full of his notes, papers, journals. My plan was to gather a selection of the best pieces—finished or unfinished—and then bind them. Five or six copies to give out as Christmas gifts to the family. *A Selection of Works from the Historic Journals of Grampa Lou*. I was actually very excited. I mean, who knew where this project could go? If the pieces turned out to be even slightly brilliant—maybe I'd seek out a publisher.

By the way, I don't want to pretend like I *knew* Grampa Lou. I didn't. All I have is a lot of vague facts about him from family members. He never got along well with Dad (his son). He was quiet, stoic, conservative. He lived through the Depression, which must have been the defining period of his life. According to my father, he didn't trust anybody and worried that at any moment he could lose everything to thieves, the government, bureaucrats. He'd lose his house, wife, children, life savings. And then he'd have to start again from nothing.

"Tight as a drum!" my father said.

But the truth? Deep down, Grampa Lou was probably a closet Marxist and definitely a romantic. I found it ironic that someone who secretly believed in socialism would end up owning and running the biggest chain of men's clothing stores in Philadelphia.

I believe the reality of these journals hurt my father deeply after we'd found them. He'd certainly built up resentment for the guy by that point—but to find out that Grampa had a heart but never showed it to him was unforgivable.

Three days earlier.

Gramma Lou sat downstairs in her big bear chair, nodding in and out of talk shows. She had been married to Grampa for forty-two years. Never married again after he died. Never even considered it. Since high school, she'd been reminding me monthly about my commitment to go through the journals. Clearly, she had an idea about what was in them.

The trunks were old, waxy, burnt-brown steamer trunks—covered with dust. Aged, yellowing paper taped to them had "L.D." written in magic marker.

The journals dated consistently from 1932–1955 and then sporadically: 1957, 1959, 1960, '62, '65, '69, '70. They stopped a couple of pages into 1970 and then that was the end of it. All told there were about thirty journals. The first few years were several notebooks apiece.

My fantasy was that I would start reading and immediately be overwhelmed—not just by the brilliance and richness of the material—but by the voice, the vision, the structure. I would marvel at not just the insight and depth of the characters—but the completeness.

My experience of the process of writing—including hundreds of fertile tenth-grade minds over the past three years—had been that in prose fragments, as in poetry, there can be a completeness. An ability to successfully convey even a single image or thought can define a person. So, I approached these papers with a healthy but restrained optimism.

Yet, after just five hours of reading, I could not have been prepared for what I discovered: Grampa Lou had *nothing* to say.

I mean, *nothing*.

I don't mean that metaphorically—like he didn't have a point of view or an imagination. I mean, literally, *nothing*.

A young man.

A young man who tries to distinguish himself.

A young man who tries to distinguish himself to the community.

Or a butcher
A butcher rides to work
by bicycle.
Wants a large family.
Can he afford it?

Through page after page, I sat frozen on the edge of my seat. Waiting. Of course, he must be building to *something*—throwing out ideas, set-ups, questions and statements—waiting for that one killer idea to come along and *BAM!* he would ride it to whatever clear conclusion it came to. But the sheer, dizzying *waiting* for something to take hold was giving me heartburn.

A man—a young man
takes a second job.

A young man and a woman from the neighborhood.

Does he know her?

At 1 a.m. I found myself suddenly rushing ahead through journal five, journal six—praying for some-thing—*anything*—to give. A full page—a paragraph—a freaking *run-on sentence*. For God sakes!

Does he know her?

Well, does he? What about that?! Does he know her? Her who? His wife? Cousin? Mistress? Which neighborhood? How young?! Does he effing know her or doesn't he?!

Why was this such a difficult question to ask?

Can he afford it?

What was stopping this seemingly devoted authorial man from writing *second* or *third* lines to his pieces? Of playing *What If?* Or simply investigating a goddamn thought? Clearly, he worked at it. He practiced. Did he resent writers? Did he think they wrote novels freehand—with no effort—no work? Was he so jealous that he was perpetually experiencing mid-sentence lockjaw? Or did he somehow believe these *were* complete?

My heart was heavy. Grampa Lou's *m.o.* was in describing stories *to be written*—characters *to be drawn*—details *to come*. It was all perpetual preparation.

I didn't know what to do.

I got back to my parents' house around two in the morning and fell asleep, wired on Grampa Lou. Ten hours of first lines repeated over and over in my head, deliriously, like some warped programming code. *Images of a man—a butcher—perpetually coming to the door with flowers—looking for—her?—a second job?—tipping his hat—holding a bicycle—a résumé—flowers—Grampa Lou—*

Over and over and over.

The next day.

In our kitchen Mom dyed marshmallow and oatmeal clusters green to look like little Christmas wreaths. I sat eating cereal—drinking coffee—in my bathrobe. It was three in the afternoon.

"Are you sleeping okay?" she asked. "Is the bed okay? That's decaf. You don't want that. Let me brew you a fresh—"

"Decaf is fine. Really."

She bumped the counter suddenly and a little green oatmeal wreath plummeted to its death.

"Mom. Everything's fine. Really. I just got to sleep late."

She began angrily jiggling red sprinkles onto the green clusters.

"You're still working on that thing?"

"Mm."

"I think you're wasting your time."

". . . and here we go."

"Your father read it all years ago. He said there just wasn't anything there."

"When does Dottie get here?" I asked, changing the subject.

"Tomorrow. Around five. You're here for such a short time. Why waste your vacation in that attic? I hate the way she pesters you to—"

"She's not pestering me. It was my idea."

"Irmey," she says, looking at me, sadly, with fingers caked in plastery green, "I liked Grampa Lou. Honestly. He was always very decent to me. But the man couldn't spell his name."

And then I didn't want to be there anymore. I knew Dottie would eventually cheer me up. But I didn't want to wait. What I wanted to do—what I wanted was to *call Joel*—but I'd spent the last twelve months learning to bury that feeling as deeply as possible. That desperation.

Back at Gramma's.

"You did say you'd read through them, right, Gram?"

"Of course. What a marvelous mind he had! Don't you think?!"

"Was there a particular year you liked? Do you remember? Or a particular period where he, y'know, took off? Or—or—or—finished something? I mean, maybe I'm missing something?"

"I think the late thirties were really very good."

"Really? What was your favorite piece?"

"Oh, I can't pick! There's just so much! And besides, that's *your* job."

Job. If he was one of my tenth-grade students I'd've graded him: *Incomplete.* And then sent an angry note to his parents.

"You really loved him, didn't you, Gram?"

She looked at me, sad but sincerely.

"Oh . . . terribly, sweetheart."

I shuddered, suddenly, thinking whatever she felt for him, would I *ever* feel this? For *anyone?*

"Honey?" she said. "Do you want some ice cream?"

A young woman drives an expensive car.

A couple on a picnic.

Jesus, why was this even bothering me so much?

A quiet Sunday morning in a park.

This wasn't about *me*. I *had* a life! I *did* get published! This was about Grampa Lou's legacy.

A man is an engineer.

A man is an engineer.

A man is an engineer.

By the end of night two, I had gotten through all the journals. Continuing was less difficult. Because I was no longer looking for greatness. I was reading purely by force of will. Just to say that I did it. That I had completed my mission.

There were no surprises. Things did not get progressively better as I neared the end. If anything, they got even less focused. At least, in the early papers there seemed to be some yearning to try to say something. By the time the journals reached 1970 there was the sense that it was time to pack it in.

I thought—*at what point do you do that?* Stop looking forward and say, *this is pointless. I need to relax now and get on with my life.*

Who knew he'd have a stroke within three years? And then die six months after that? Would it have changed anything? Would he have done things differently? Stopped writing earlier?

I did not want to judge him. I couldn't. I mean, who the hell was I to go through this man's life, anyway? Now I was going to give a "report" to the family?! And I heard my mother's voice saying, *Well, we all knew it was going to turn out this way, didn't we? What a waste of time.*

Just thinking like that made me angry. And so—

And so, I did the only thing I could do. I started over. Started reading all of it all over again right from the beginning. Seeing if I missed anything. Seeing if there was anything to salvage. I looked at all of it. All of it.

In my exhaustion, I found myself continually focusing on his . . . his

doodles.

You know. His little curlicues and half-shapes and trapezoids decorating the margins. And sometimes not even in the margins. Occasionally, when he seemed particularly stuck—some design would *explode* into the very middle of a page like grotesque punctuations of his writerly frustrations.

Doodles. Swirls. Cross-hatches. Marks and lines taking up centimeters in the gutters of the page. At least they were what? Finished?

198 | **Miserable Holiday Stories**

I went through the journals again—but this time looking for some kind of—I don't know—artistic doodle progression.

Maybe there was one. Somehow, as the years rolled by, the doodles did seem to actually become—more *florid*? More detailed with flourishing spirals—crashing tides, waterfall branches. But always tangential, always alongside his fractured, undelivered thoughts.

Was he saying something in pictures that he couldn't in prose? Were these his expressions of joy? Frustration? Disappointment? Were his hard, dark lines actually expressing anger and rage?

I laid out the strongest—most elaborate pages—side-by-side on the attic floor. Years, decades of history, a world revolving—and tried to take it all in. It was almost like sheet music—this symphony of swoops and gullies, slashes and cascades. Ovals within ovals. Marginal fireworks—followed by stationary lines of peace and contentment.

Is this what Gramma was seeing? Were these the real stories? And did they move me?

I wanted to be moved. Simply because I needed to finish this. Yet, I knew deep down that this *wasn't* art. It couldn't be. *Everyone* doodles. *I doodle.* Were these doodles really better than anyone else's? Of course not. But now who was being hypocritical? I mean I would've collected his prose fragments and called that literature. Why should his doodles be any different?

My objective was always to see what Gramma saw. To feel what she felt and share that with others. Couldn't doodles convey a feeling? A state of mind?

Of course, they could.

There *was* beauty and expression here.

I saw it.

I felt it.

That night, I dreamt of Daliesque doodle streets, buildings, people with lines extending off their heads and arms and hair. A doodle room with a doodle bed watching doodle Joel—lying naked with doodle hair and his new doodle girlfriend. Running his hand through her hair—a spaghetti of inky black strands that curled and wisped around his fingers like a cat's cradle. They shimmered— out of focus—in doodle lines that got darker as cross-hatching and definition were heaped upon them and growing, growing.

Christmas Eve.

Dad brings home Gramma Lou, who marvels at Mom's over-the-top decorations and then plants herself in front of the TV and quickly falls asleep.

Dottie and Mark finally arrive around seven, held up by traffic and bad weather. Dottie's beet red from the cold. Her cheeks and nose glisten and she hugs me. They almost went off the road when an eighteen-wheeler collided with a Chevy Caprice that had skidded into the wrong direction. They thought it was certain death—but got around it just as all the cars behind them slammed on their brakes. The truck straightened, but Dottie could tell—looking behind her—that cars were colliding.

Anyone would be cranky after that kind of a drive. But Dottie grins ear to ear—my puppy dog sister with her wet, runny nose—so excited to see me.

"Did you finish it?" she asks.

I flash a box holding my six bound copies.

"Cool!"

"Took me three hours at Insty-Print. I gave the packing dude with the *Duck Dynasty* beard my phone number."

Only Dottie would understand why I would do this.

"Let me see!" she says, tugging at the box.

"No!" I say, "I want to give them out at dinner!"

Dinner.

Everyone is pleasant. The box of bound volumes by my chair is not a secret and everyone humors me. But, oddly, I feel good. Great. Finished. I've completed My Quest. And now all that's left is for the Hero to bring her prize back to the community. For the second time this year, I'm free. I can officially get on with my life.

And Dottie eats voraciously, bouncing out of her seat. She keeps looking over at me, grinning, urging me to go on. But Mark stands and then reaches across the table and takes her hand.

"Tell them," he says.

Everyone stops eating. Dottie, eyes sparkling, sits up straight and says:

"*Well . . . I'm pregnant.*"

Everyone looks at one another, jaws wide, excited, out of breath. They scream. Dad stands, beaming, reaches across the table, vigorously shakes Mark's hand. Mom and Gramma both start crying. Mom hugs Dottie. Everyone is thrilled.

"When's the due date? How long? You know what you're having? We're gonna be grandparents!! We have to change the guest room! Have to get a crib!"

I'm smiling. Then I'm crying, but desperately trying not to. Desperately trying—wanting—to be part of this. To not make this about me. Because it isn't. It isn't. I hug Dottie, smiling. Everyone's looking at me. And I run out of the room.

I'm in the garage and I'm smoking after I had just quit six months ago. I'm crying and getting the cig all wet and *why did I even come home? What the hell is wrong with me? That I spent my only week of vacation locked up in a stupid, musty attic while real people—young people—with full lives are creating babies?!*

I'll never have children. How can I? Why was I drinking and crying for six months straight? Joel was my last chance. Who would want me now? Who would want this—this—forty-year-old nothing?

No. This isn't about me. I love Dottie and she should be pregnant, and she should be happy. And—

And Dottie is here. She puts an arm around me and holds me. We sit on the hood of her car and watch the snow fall in big, pillowy chunks and she hugs me—my little sister—and I'm so happy for her. I want to say that but I can't make the right words come. But it doesn't matter because she gets it. She understands.

"I thought there would be something," I say. "I thought he would leave me something *for me*. Some—I don't know—some goddamn message in there. For me, personally. To give me—*hope*. But there was nothing."

"He gave you something," she says, smiling knowingly and pushing the box of books into my arms. "He gave you gifts you still have to deliver."

So I have six bound copies of *A Selection of Works from The Historic Journals of Grampa Lou*. But they don't say that because I didn't have time to make cover pages at Insty-Print.

I leave one copy, with no introduction, to Mom and Dad—who stare at it, blankly—at a loss for how to respond. But I don't care. What they do with it is not my business. A copy also goes to Gramma Louella who seems to have no idea what I've given her—but is delighted, nonetheless. She will put it down with other books and magazines on the table near her TV. She will forget about it and sleep.

Then, Dottie, Mark and I pile ourselves and three more bound copies of the book into Mark's car. We anonymously drop off copies at a homeless shelter run by St. Ann's church, the 23rd Police Precinct, and finally the office of *The Market Courier*—the smallest local paper in

Philadelphia. We give them the books as Christmas gifts, drop-offs with no identification—no questions asked. All recipients take the copies eagerly—happy to receive all things at Christmastime. The homeless will have something to look at while they eat. Overnight DWI guests at the precinct may glance at the book and sober up quicker. And the weekend edition of the *Courier* will do what no one has ever done—*print one of Grampa's doodles*—one of the smaller, more expressive ones, anonymously, on the cover of its Arts Section.

And at long last, Grampa Lou will be published.

Dropping off these books with Dottie and Mark—who egg me on with their unflappable good cheer through rainy, slush-covered streets, joyously ruining our clothes—is a warm, cathartic moment that has now become my all-time favorite Christmas memory. At least for the present.

The final bound copy I will bring back west. But not for me, for my students. I want them to experience an act of pure expression on whatever level they choose to take it. If it inspires them in some way, great. If it is a bizarre joke to them—or just utterly meaningless—

well, that's okay, too.

Yes, I still feel like I'm riding on a wagon with three good wheels and one broken one. Forever bouncing across the landscape. Not sure if or when the rest of the wagon's going to collapse out from under me. But holding on, tightly, knowing that three good wheels are still better than most people could ask for.

And I'm looking forward to my date Sunday night.

With the dude with the beard.

From Insty-Print.

Maggie

JEFF AND MAGGIE WALK OUT ONTO CENTER STAGE and meet in the middle. He hands her some papers.

JEFF: Here.

She looks through the pages and is touched.

MAGGIE: You wrote this for me?

JEFF: I did.

MAGGIE: Thank you.

She hugs him. She freezes. He turns to the audience.

JEFF: This is Maggie—the first girl I ever really liked at college—and the first one I ever wrote anything for. It's a Christmas story. It's pretty good, too. I really made an effort. I desperately wanted to get together with Maggie, but she had a boyfriend within the first week of college. (*to Maggie, who unfreezes*) You know he doesn't care about you at all?

MAGGIE: I know.

JEFF: I mean—where is he? He's never around. He acts like he owns you!

MAGGIE: I know.

JEFF: So, dump him. Go out with me!

MAGGIE: I can't. I'm committed.

JEFF: Why?!

MAGGIE: I love him.

JEFF: You haven't known him for more than three weeks!

MAGGIE: I know. Seems longer, doesn't it?

She freezes. He turns to audience.

JEFF: Her boyfriend, Billy, is short, wimpy and needy. But he's artistic, kind of cool. Blah blah blah. She mothers him a lot, which is probably why it works for them.

MAGGIE: (*to audience, unfreezing*) The neediness is kind of cute, though!

JEFF: (*to audience*) No, it's not. It's repulsive. Eventually, she breaks up with Billy—but we still never end up going out. (*to Maggie*) Since when do you like girls?

MAGGIE: It's just where I am right now.

JEFF: So, what was up with Billy?

MAGGIE: That was different.

JEFF: We're never going to happen, are we?

MAGGIE: Never say never!

JEFF: (*to audience and Maggie*) But we never did go out. And now we're both middle-aged and have kids with other people. Life goes on.

MAGGIE: (*to audience and Jeff*) But we're friends on Facebook! Poke!

The Unbreakable Toy

EVERYONE KNOWS, OF COURSE, THAT TOY MAKING IS *BIG business.*

As the world's toy needs grew exponentially in the new century, young eager toymakers flocked to secluded Bandersnatch Valley, Utah, with its lush vegetation and peerless climate, where leviathan toy factories, cities unto themselves really, seemed to pop up out of the landscape like hyperactive mole rats. Companies with names like *Stuff'nFun, HappyPlastic, FunJunk!, MessAbound, Clownside, Funz-A-Bruin, ThingsThatSpin, Flurflang, RUBE, InkBlot, CarbonFeetprint, eFunji, ExplodingDoh, Newgat, LiederFunen, Slippery'nWet, Nerdelveis, SmileOrElse, DollAddict,* and the biggest mega-toy company of them all—*The Big Old Fun and Frolic Organization*—or *BOFFO.*

As decades of expansive growth continued, a new generation of toy makers were born right into these factory-cities. And some scientists believed that this new generation's ears had evolved to become just a *tiny bit pointy*—making them look slightly but not quite *like elves*.

But of course, they weren't elves. They were toy makers—with hopes, dreams, heartbreak and back pain—just like you and me.

Also quite like the hero of our story, young Gimlet Starbuck.

It was "New Toy Day" at BOFFO—that day in mid-November that would determine which new toy would rule supreme over the upcoming holiday season—and Gimlet Starbuck, a good-natured, if opaque, young lad, was running late for his new toy presentation. Currently, Gimlet was being rejected by his heart's desire, Ophelia Finkelstein, the beautiful company Plooze Queen, who knew deep down inside that she was destined for greater things.

Plooze, of course—or Plastic Ooze, as it was originally conceived—a super synthetic compound which came in liquid, powder, or filament form—was the manufacturing cornerstone for all modern toy companies. A person in the elite position of *Executive Director of Plooze Controls* was typically responsible for ensuring that Plooze inventory was high and that all of the machinery that required Plooze—from locomotive-sized machines to simple desktop 4D Printers—were maintained with a steady, healthy supply. At BOFFO, Ophelia had reached the extraordinarily high position of *Special Assistant Director of Plooze Continuity*. But most people simply referred to her as the Plooze Queen.

Darting from department to department to maintain Plooze inventory, berating those who wasted it and rewarding those who used it most efficiently (with extra Plooze), Ophelia knew that it was *she* who truly ran BOFFO.

Upon seeing her that morning, Gimlet's thoughts went like this: *gosh, she's cute. I hope I don't have any gross stains on my shirt*.

"How are you this morning, Ophelia?! You're looking terrifically professional—or uh—professionally terrific today! I hope you have a—an absolutely terrific day!" he said, pathetically clasping his oversized black bag to his waist. "Because—because that would be terrific!"

"Need Plooze?" she asked, icily.

"No. But, uhm, perhaps we could discuss Plooze over an afternoon snack? Possibly? Or not? Or maybe? Either is really okay."

"That sounds exceptional, Gimlet. However, I'm afraid I never fraternize with coworkers. But do let me know if your Plooze needs change."

Now, if things seemed not quite perfect for Gimlet at this point, they certainly didn't improve when Sozgüd Klaw appeared. Sozgüd was BOFFO's current toy-making ace.

"Well, hel-lo, Ophelia! How's Plooze?!" said Sozgüd, flashing a crystalline white smile.

"Sozgüd!"

Of all the BOFFO toy makers, only Sozgüd could make Ophelia momentarily forget Plooze.

"Need Plooze?" she asked, not completely forgetting Plooze.

Sozgüd Klaw was bright, rich, charming, well-dressed, cultured, and had just the right amount of hair, which was always styled from the trendiest social hubs. And most importantly, he *always* made the most excellent toys. For the past six years, Sozgüd's toys had won Best New Toy, outshining all others. His toys were expensive, modern, and cool, and dominated every holiday season. All the other toy makers, Gimlet included, strove year after year to design toys to defeat Sozgüd. But year after year, they failed. Because they—like Gimlet—were failures.

"Your *eyes* are like Plooze, Ophelia!" said Sozgüd. "The deeper one looks, the deeper one falls into that weird, dark, plasticy stuff!"

"*Sozgüd!*" she said, swooning and fraternizing.

Gimlet shuffled with his bag, thinking he might barf at any moment.

"But I've got to go!" said Sozgüd. "I've got a *Brilliant Idea!*"

"Are you presenting for New Toy Day?" she asked.

"Of course," replied Sozgüd, "I did say I've got a *Brilliant Idea!*"

"I've got something, too!" squeaked Gimlet, clutching his bag. Effortlessly, they ignored him.

But this time, Gimlet really *did* have something. He'd put great care and thought into this one. It was good. He knew it. Maybe not great. Certainly, better than the last one, which was really the pits. Perhaps not the Eiffel Tower of toys, but a really *real* good toy. With this almost certainly pretty-good-toy, he *knew* things were about to change. He sensed it. He *felt* it. And maybe, if he won New Toy Day, Ophelia and everyone else would finally look up to him for the great toymaker that he knew he could be.

Suddenly, Gimlet wanted terribly to give Ophelia a quick glimpse of his wonderful new toy. But as he began lifting it out of its bag, Sozgüd abruptly swiveled toward the presentation room, knocking into him. With this collision, Gimlet's new toy flew into the air, somersaulted three times and came to land, *KERSPLASH* into a nearby cleaning bucket.

"*Nitwit!*" snapped Sozgüd and he disappeared into the presentation room.

Gimlet ran to the bucket and retrieved his toy. It was completely soaked. He wiped at it with his shirt sleeve, but there was something sticky in the bucket that was now hardening quickly. Even the place on Gimlet's shirt where he wiped was hardening. But he had no time to lose. Soaked or not, he had to make that meeting!

The presentation room was crammed with hundreds of toy makers and dozens upon dozens of toys: adorable dolls, cryptic games, surreal figurines, blank dice, interlocking pieces of marble and shale, talking furry gremlins, toys that grabbed and kicked and belched smoke, and incomprehensible digital toys that required you to do nothing but stare at them for hours.

And the toy makers! Youthful, restless, and awkward, with strange haircuts and wide, spin-art ties! And all trying desperately to impress the *Grand Administrative Toymaker!*

Currently, a young, goateed toy maker named Rollo Cotati was presenting. Rollo was an excitable lad whose toy ideas never seemed quite finished. He and Gimlet were best friends and housemates.

"Well, it's just the most spectacular thing!" Rollo told the GAT. "It's unique! It's fun! And it's new, new, NEW!!"

That was always the most basic precept of New Toy Day. Every toy endeavored to be "New, New, NEW!" Most weren't. Most were not-even-cleverly-rehashed toys from previous holiday seasons.

Rollo whipped the covering from his toy, and there it was: something resembling a small, brownish loaf of not-completely-cooked rye bread. Sozgüd smirked. The GAT looked on, bored.

"What is it?" he yawned.

"I call it: *The Hairy Loaf!*" Rollo said, waving and blinking excitedly.

"Hairy?" asked the GAT.

Everyone nudged closer to look, and yes, there actually were tiny, black hairs all over the thing. It was quite odd.

"Let me tell you how I came up with it!" Rollo exploded.

"Please don't," replied the GAT. The GAT never wanted to know toy maker secrets. They bugged him.

"So—what's it do?" he asked, impatiently.

"Well, everyone loves to make bread, right? And what's the best part of making bread? Why the *kneading,* the *thumping* of the dough! Am I right?"

The GAT squinted and sighed. Rollo began frantically punching and squeezing his loaf, his hands sinking freely into its gunky mass. Each time he removed his hands, the loaf came back to its original, uncooked, Rye loaf-like shape. Gimlet looked on, impressed. It actually did look fun.

"Y'see," continued Rollo, excitedly, "you can have hours and hours of kneading and pounding the Hairy Loaf just like you would a real loaf! It's always, *always* fun!"

The GAT snorted.

"How *many* hours and hours?"

"More than two!" Rollo replied.

"More than three?" the GAT asked.

"More than two and a quarter!" gulped Rollo, hopefully.

"And then what? It hardens like a real loaf?"

All eyes were on Rollo. He trembled, nervously, and scratched at his goatee. Sweat danced on his brow.

"Uh . . . yes."

The GAT leaned forward.

"So, except for the hair——" said the GAT, "and no, I don't want to know how that got there——how *exactly* is this different from a *real* loaf of bread?"

"Well——I——I wouldn't suggest *eating* it," gurgled Rollo.

Two large security guards stepped toward Rollo. Rollo beseeched the GAT.

"Wait! Wait! We could call it *The Inedible Loaf*! That's new, new, NEW! That's——"

The guards sidled up to Rollo. Smartly, he receded into the crowd. The GAT looked at his chart.

"Sozgüd Klaw!" he announced.

Sozgüd stepped forward, and a buoyant smile erupted from the GAT's face.

"Ah, Sozgüd! Our exemplary toy maker!"

Sozgüd bowed, graciously. The GAT noticed he'd come empty-handed.

"You——do have a toy, Sozgüd?" he asked.

"I do," replied Sozgüd, confidently. "But this toy is unlike any toy that has ever come before you! You'll commend its complexity! Yet its simplicity is sublime!"

A collective gasp filled the room. The GAT sat on the edge of his seat. *He's going to do it, again!* thought Gimlet. Sozgüd spread his arms wide.

"I give you," he cried, "*The Brilliant Idea*!"

Everyone waited.

Nothing happened.

Sozgüd stood perfectly still. The GAT stared, his eyebrows ruffling, confused.

"Is that it?" asked the GAT.

Sozgüd's arms fell to his sides. His grin remained.

"That's it," he said.

Gimlet's heart raced. *Could this be Sozgüd's first failure?!* But suddenly, Sozgüd leapt forward at the GAT, pointing and gesturing, excitedly.

"Don't you see?! *This is the very essence of toys!* And not just *toys,* mind you . . . but *everything! The Brilliant Idea!* Now, for a modest price, you, too, can have your very own *Brilliant Idea* to enjoy through the holiday festivities and beyond!"

Coughs and "mmphs" rose from the crowd. But Sozgüd spun on them, with a fury.

"Now! You might say, well, *anyone* can have an idea! Certainly, I look around here and see dozens upon dozens of ideas! But how many of them are *Brilliant?!*"

The toy makers looked at each other, disheartened. It was true. There really wasn't anything even in the farthest reaches of brilliance with this bunch, although Rollo frantically waved his *Hairy Loaf.*

"But now," continued Sozgüd, grinning, "there can be *Brilliance* for everyone! *At a price!*"

One toy maker with particularly pointy ears raised a hand.

"But how can you sell an idea?" he asked.

"Tosh pish!" replied Sozgüd. "That's the easy part! Anyone can sell anything! You should all know that!"

"And how can you ensure *brilliance*?" asked another with slightly nubbier ears.

"*With this!*" Sozgüd shouted, whipping out a gold decal from his vest pocket. "A *Certificate of Brilliancy* included in every package!"

The crowd leaned forward and "ooooohed."

"But is it *fun*?" asked Rollo. "A toy's supposed to be fun!"

"It's more fun than your loaf!" called an obese, bearded toy maker.

"It's—it's a thinking toy! Like a chess piece or a jigsaw puzzle!" said a short toy maker with a voice like a frog.

"It's the *Idea* that's important!" said a toy maker with a foreign accent that no one could discern.

"But . . . what if their ideas *aren't* Brilliant?" asked Gimlet, vaguely assertive.

Sozgüd whirled on Gimlet.

"But they *will* be, Gimlet. Don't you see? That *is* the toy. You buy the toy and you're buying the very *permission* to be Brilliant!"

He turned to the toy makers with a look of complete conviction.

"Every man, woman, and child alive has Brilliance. But from the moment they're born, it just sits there, gathering dust, never being used. Think of it! How many of you have ever actually given yourselves the permission to be Brilliant?"

The toy makers looked down at their shoes, shamefully. Sozgüd smiled.

"Exactly."

He turned, once again, to the GAT.

"But now, your GATfulness, we will *give* them permission. And make a healthy yuletide profit to boot!"

Sozgüd finished and stepped back, confidently. The room was silent. Gimlet watched, fearfully. The GAT stared at Sozgüd, impressed.

"Why, that's . . . that's . . . *Brilliant!*" yelled the GAT, rising suddenly from his enormous chair. (And he never rose.) "Three cheers for Sozgüd!"

"Hip hip, hooray!" cheered the toy makers, dubiously.

Gimlet watched, thinking *it isn't even a proper toy. Would any child want to unwrap a box and find an "Idea" inside? Yet, I should probably be the first in line to get one.*

The herd of toy makers stood and began shuffling toward the exit. The GAT took a final look at his chart.

"Hold on!" he shouted, and everyone froze. "It seems we've got one last, late arrival!"

He turned and gazed at Gimlet, who clutched at his bag, nervously.

"You there! Gumdrop!"

"Gimlet, sir."

"Well! Whatever you've got—is it Brilliant?!" the GAT asked, sharply.

"No!" cried Gimlet. "I mean—well—well . . ."

The GAT's face turned pink. He leaned toward Gimlet.

"C'mon! C'mon! We haven't got all day!"

Gimlet inched forward and withdrew his toy. Everyone looked on, curiously. Many covered their mouths, suppressing giggles. Gimlet's toy was a great, horrific, poorly assembled mess of a thing—made of bells, strings, baubles, and gum. Its body was a column of poorly arranged popsicle sticks, with a multicolored pinwheel leading from its neck and, finally, a great horn pasted badly at the top. Since falling in the bucket, though, it did have a curious *shine* to it. Indeed, Gimlet, in his own way, was quite proud of this mess. While yes, it wasn't the most attractive toy he'd ever made—it did look kind of neat, especially when it was all lit up and the pinwheel was spinning. Of course, he hadn't actually lit it up or spun the pinwheel as yet, but he was fairly certain that if it did light and spin, then, yes, it would probably be pretty neat.

"What do you call it?" the GAT asked.

"Well, it's . . . uhm . . . it's a—" Gimlet floundered. Building the thing had taken so much time, that naming it had never occurred to him. "It's—"

"*It's a Gimlet!*" shouted one toy maker, laughing.

"Yes! A *Gimlet!*" cackled another and the room erupted in guffaws.

Red-faced, Gimlet stood his ground.

"Yes," he said, matter-of-factly. "It's a *Gimlet.*"

"Named it after yourself, did you, Gangrene?"

"Gimlet, sir."

"And what's it do?" asked the GAT, impatiently.

"Do?"

Gimlet fumbled in his jacket for the batteries. It didn't do much, but if he could just turn it on . . . He started perspiring. Where were those . . . *there!*

"Here we go!" he said.

He slapped the batteries into the center cylinder (made of double-hardened Plooze) and pressed a button on the middle of the pinwheel. He waited. Nothing happened. He spun the pinwheel by hand trying to jump-start it.

Nothing. It was that weird coating from the bucket! It had somehow frozen everything in place. His perspiration grew heavier.

"It—it worked last night!" he fibbed.

The GAT gnashed his teeth and grumbled.

"Wait! Wait! It spins!" he cried, pushing at the edge of the pinwheel. But the entire spinning mechanism was stuck. All Gimlet had was a polished, frozen, worthless mess.

"That's it! I've seen enough!" called the GAT.

The guards moved towards Gimlet. Gimlet stared at his toy, frustrated and enraged. *All that work! All that hope! Why couldn't* he *be Brilliant?!* Bitterly, he flung the toy to the ground with all his might—

and it bounced

—and then fell back into his hand in one smooth motion, as gentle as a feather.

A hush fell over the room; everyone stared, astonished. Sozgüd's mouth fell open. Gimlet himself stared at the toy. It had *never* done that before.

"Do—that—again," said the GAT sitting forward in his chair, eyes wide.

Nervously, Gimlet flung his toy to the ground. Again, it bounced back up and fell gently back into his hand. And then he did it once more and again the same thing happened.

"How does it do that?" asked the GAT.

"Uhm," said Gimlet. "That's the secret!" Which was true, because it was a secret to him, too.

"May I see it?" asked the GAT.

Gimlet carefully handed the toy to the GAT, who held it up and turned and pondered and examined it, trying to unlock its mystery. Then, suddenly, with all his might, he flung it at the toy makers! The toy makers ducked, quickly, as the Gimlet shot across their heads, crashed into the far wall and bounced, effortlessly, back into the hand of the elderly GAT, who stared at the toy, astonished.

"Give it a spin!" called out Rollo.

"A spin? Oh—yes!" he replied.

And the GAT threw it high into the air with a flicking motion that caused it to flip over on itself. While spinning, suddenly, the multicolors of the pinwheel flew about and the horn blew in a sweet, surprising way! The *Gimlet* bounced off the ceiling, ricocheted off two toymakers and fell, like a snowflake, back into the GAT's hand. He smiled, pleased. And the real Gimlet's eyes widened, stunned.

"*It bounces!*" said the GAT.

"Well—I mean—yes," agreed Gimlet.

The toy makers *cheered*. Some threw their own toys to the ground, in hopes of finding heretofore unknown bounceability. Rollo threw his loaf to the ground, but it merely collapsed with an unripe *SPLAT!*

Sozgüd, disgruntled, stepped forward.

"Balls bounce," he said.

The GAT thought on this.

"That's true," he said, and then looked, questioningly at Gimlet. "Bouncing isn't new. So, what's *new* about this thing?"

"Well—well, you see, then," babbled Gimlet.

"Perhaps . . . it's unbreakable?" sneered Sozgüd.

The GAT looked at Gimlet.

"Is it?" he asked.

"It—yes," Gimlet replied, swallowing fearfully. "It is."

"We shall see!" said Sozgüd. And he snatched the toy from the GAT and threw it forcefully to the crowd.

"Go on!" he called, malevolently, to the toy makers. "Break it! If you can!"

The toy makers swarmed upon the toy.

As all good toy makers knew—*this* was the ultimate test of a toy. Never had there been a toy which couldn't be broken! Breakage was the exact reason for the existence of toy makers in the first place. *Toys broke.* Ergo, someone had to make new ones.

With great glee and fervor, the toymakers set about attempting to dismantle the thing. Not just because they wished to find its weakness, but because they hardly ever got the chance to break toys themselves! Being asked to destroy a toy—*especially someone else's*—was fun!

They leapt up and down on the misshapen thing, attempting to stomp it to the ground. They pulled and pulled, trying to tear it apart! They tried to crack it with a hammer and cut it with shears. But nothing could break the toy.

"*I'll break it!*" cried Sozgüd, grabbing the toy back, furiously. He threw himself atop it, tearing at it with his hands and swinging it around, frantically. But all that did was make the horn toot louder.

"*Sozgüd!*" the GAT called out. "*Enough!*"

Exhausted and dripping with sweat, Sozgüd returned the toy to the GAT, who then turned, most seriously, to Gimlet.

"Goober," he began.

"Gimlet, sir," interrupted Gimlet.

"Never in my sixty-eight years have I seen a toy that would not break! Truly, this remarkable invention . . . is new!"

"*New!*" erupted the toymakers. "*New! New! NEW!*"

"I must think on this, Gorgo," said the GAT.

"Gim—never mind," said Gimlet.

"But I commend you!" continued the GAT. "This could well be a winner!"

"Huzzah!" shouted the toy makers and they rushed to Gimlet and lifted him up onto their shoulders. Gimlet, smiled, astonished. For the first time that he could remember, his heart was filled with joy.

"Congratulations, Gimlet," said a familiar voice oozing with honey at the back of the room. It was Ophelia, dangling an empty Plooze cartridge. She smiled at him. *Him!* Surely, this was a day to remember.

Sozgüd, infuriated, pointed a stern finger at the GAT.

"*Don't you forget my Idea!*" he snarled. "*It's Brilliant!*" And with that, he lurched out of the room.

That evening, Gimlet returned to his tiny apartment at Bungalow 37 of Lysander Hills, a gated community, reasonably priced, with living quarters established for all the BOFFO employees and their families. Or, as in Gimlet's case, Rollo, five other young toy makers, and Gimlet's best friend, Midge.

Midge and Gimlet had known each other since childhood, when her parents, Moe and Ida, mysteriously disappeared in an international civic improvement accident.

Years earlier, Midge's parents had become famous as *Perfectionists* known throughout the world for their ability to improve almost anything. (A trait they passed on to Midge.)

They had started as mere amateur Perfectionists, spending most of their time re-setting friends' off-balance picture frames and correcting minor grammatical errors in fancy restaurant menus. As their celebrity grew, they decided to fully incorporate themselves as *Professional Perfectionists, LLC (PPL)*.

PPL started small, advising on things like straightening crooked highways and stabilizing bridges that swayed a little too much in the breeze. Shortly, they were hired for their most prestigious job—to go to the exotic but backward nation of Adanac and advise the government on how to effectively turn things forward again.

It was an undertaking expected to last at least a year. Not wanting to sidetrack Midge's education, they unselfishly left her in the care of their good friends and euchre partners, Gimlet's parents. One day, however, after she'd lived with Gimlet for a few years, Midge received the awful news that her parents had been swallowed whole while excavating for an Adanacian canyon refilling project.

As time passed, Midge gave up hope of ever seeing her parents again and she relaxed into the pleasant but mediocre life of living with Gimlet and his family. She grew fond of Gimlet. And so, years later, when he sent word to her that he and Rollo's new employer, BOFFO, had all sorts of weak corners and minor equipment blemishes that could really use the efforts of a natural-born Perfectionist, she was thrilled to join them at Lysander Hills.

Now, as Gimlet, Rollo and their toy maker roommates all returned from the factory, cheerfully honking the horns on their electric scooters, Midge knew good news was in the air.

"*Gimlet's won New Toy Day!*" called Rollo.

"Really?!" said Midge.

"Well, not quite yet," said Gimlet. "It's still being decided."

"Oh, you've won for sure, I bet!" said Midge and she hugged Gimlet almost too affectionately.

"What's that?" she said, noticing the cleaning bucket dangling from his hand.

"Oh—I—I thought I'd help you make the place just a little more perfect!" said Gimlet, thinking quickly.

And Midge's eyes lit up.

Gimlet dashed up to his room and quietly closed the door. He had managed to sneak the bucket of cleaning liquid that his toy had fallen into, out of the factory at the last possible second. But he still hadn't had a chance to examine it. Now, finally alone in his room, he knelt down to take a look. There, near the bottom of the bucket was a tiny label which read: SEALANT.

Sealant? thought Gimlet. That made a sort-of sense but surely that wouldn't have made his toy unbreakable, would it?

"Ready?" called a spry voice.

Gimlet looked up. Midge, with a stack of sponges, stood in his doorway, exuberantly.

"Of course," said Gimlet, quickly shoving the bucket out of sight behind his bed. "Y'know, Midge, I think she really noticed me today!"

"Who?" asked Midge.

"Ophelia!" said Gimlet, heading down the stairs.

"Oh," said Midge, disheartened.

A bit later, as they scrubbed away at a particularly grimy section of the kitchen sink's underbelly, Rollo ran in, bellowing.

"*You've won, Gimlet!* You've won New Toy Day! Your *Unbreakable Gimlet* is headed for production! You're going to be the hit of the holidays!"

"Oh, Gimlet! That's wonderful!" cheered Midge.

But Gimlet had dropped his sponge and fainted dead away.

Things moved fast.

The very next day, *Unbreakable Gimlets!* went into triple-heavy production for the holiday season. It was the GAT's idea to have Gimlet himself demonstrate the new toy—bouncing and twirling it—in all of their new yuletide commercials. Additionally, Gimlet was given strict oversight of all *Gimlet* production, which was good, because he was anxious about providing any access to his special *Magical Non-Breaking Formula*, especially since he still had no idea why it worked.

One thing he discovered was that regular buckets of sealant did not make toys unbreakable. He learned this when he tried dipping some of his *Gimlet* toys in those buckets and they broke apart almost immediately. Yet a single drop from his one original bucket—mixed with *any* liquid—seemed to render his toys utterly impervious to harm.

To keep his secret under wraps, Gimlet found himself dressing up in terrible disguises and sneaking around the plant late at night, after all the other toymakers had gone to sleep. He would then put scant drops of his original liquid into the gigantic manufacturing vats of normal sealant. Fortunately, the GAT trusted Gimlet and never asked about the whys and wherefores of his toy production. As long as Gimlet kept cranking out thousands of copies of the *Toy That Can't Be Broken!* the GAT was satisfied.

Soon, the holiday shopping season was in full bloom and novelty stores and merchants couldn't keep the toys on their shelves. Everyone wanted an *Unbreakable Gimlet*. Adults, children. Young people showed them off at parties and the elderly stared at them for hours, smiling. Suddenly, Gimlet was a celebrity. He received calls to appear on talk shows and newscasts. One TV station had him fly high across the city in a weather balloon, dropping *Gimlets* out to see how high they could bounce.

The more the toys sold, the more Gimlet had to make, and the more and more profits kept pouring in to BOFFO.

One night in mid-December, the GAT himself arrived at Bungalow 37 with two large, heavy-set businessmen in impressive hand-tailored suits and top hats—*Mr. Throttle* and *Mr. Clutch*. Throttle and Clutch were the true owners of BOFFO and after all the recent media attention, they were eager to meet their famous toy maker. Throttle and Clutch informed Gimlet that they were officially promoting him to the rank of *Essential Special Toymaker, Second Class*, and moving him directly into the Manufacturing Plant itself—into the *Essential Special* suites—so that he could increase *Gimlet* production even further as the happiest holiday neared.

"Thank you both so much!" said Gimlet, shaking their hands. But then he pulled back, reluctantly. "It's just—"

"What?" said Clutch.

"I'm honored, sir. But—I'm afraid I can't do it."

"Why not?" asked Throttle.

"What's the problem?" asked Clutch.

"Well—Rollo and Midge and I—we all came up together—and well—"

"Tut tut!" said Throttle.

"*Bring them!*" said Clutch. "They can help with production!"

Gimlet turned, hopefully, to his friends. But they were already gone.

"*Rollo?! Midge?!*"

He heard a *CLUNKING* noise from upstairs.

"We're packing!" Midge called out, excitedly.

Gimlet breathed a sigh of relief.

That night, the three friends moved into the factory. They took residence in the most exquisite suites they'd ever seen, packed with the finest foods, the smartest clothes and furniture so modern it didn't even make sense. Quickly, they settled in and unpacked and with the constant background hum of heavy machinery, their new home was truly cozy.

Late that first evening, they awoke to a strange scratching sound coming from the kitchen. Cautiously, they tiptoed in and there, hunched over and quivering in the corner, near the stove, was Sozgüd, dilapidated and defeated. In his arms, he cradled dozens of impressively packaged *Brilliant Ideas*.

"*They've kicked me out!*" he moaned.

"But what about your Idea?" asked Rollo, knowing that Sozgüd's *Brilliant Idea* had shipped right alongside the *Unbreakable Gimlet*—though in considerably fewer numbers.

"No one's buying them!" urped Sozgüd. "And the ones that sold are being returned by the cartload! Everyone's saying it's *not a toy!!*"

He grabbed desperately at Gimlet's nightshirt.

"It's a toy, isn't it?! Isn't it?! A good toy?! Not a *Gimlet!* But still!"

"Of course, it's a toy," said Gimlet, compassionately. "There, there, Sozgüd. Get hold of yourself."

But Sozgüd's head darted to and fro, nerve-wracked and paranoid.

"*They're after me, you know!*"

"Who?" asked Midge.

"Throttle and Clutch! The GAT! They blame me—*me!*—for the *Idea!* They want me to work overtime, triple-time, answering hate mail, begging forgiveness! They want me to go door-to-door of every house that bought a *Brilliant Idea* and drop to my knees, apologizing! *It's madness!*"

Gimlet looked at Sozgüd, trembling, and thought to himself *is that really such a terrible idea? Begging for forgiveness?*

Sozgüd leapt to the counter, shaking.

"What was that?! Did you hear them?! Hide me!"

"Hide you?" asked Rollo. "Here in the factory? It's the first place they'd look."

Suddenly, there was a light pattering of footsteps in the hallway. Sozgüd, panicked, dropped his packages and leapt out the open window.

"*They've found me!*" he cried, disappearing into the night.

Rollo, Gimlet, and Midge looked toward the door just as Wrinkles the BOFFO factory cat peered in, curiously.

Gimlet knelt down and picked up one of Sozgüd's packages.

"They weren't such bad *Brilliant Ideas*," he said.

Rollo and Midge agreed.

The next day, Gimlet went to inspect the factory operations. Since the incident with Sozgüd, he'd become anxious and began worrying that other toy makers might be prowling around his vats. That morning, he'd had the entire production staff replaced by Toy Maker Robots. And just to be doubly precautious, he began taping huge signs on the vats that read KEEP OUT! HANDS OFF! and THIS MEANS YOU!

So he was startled when a soft-as-satin voice called to him from the plant doorway.

"Hi, Gimmie!"

Gimlet turned. It was Ophelia, in a flowing, oversized lab smock that swayed magically in the artificial factory breeze.

"Ophelia!" stammered Gimlet, noticing that she carried no Plooze.

"I've been promoted!" she said, proudly. "I'm in *Cog Maintenance* now."

"That must be very exciting," returned Gimlet, swooning stupidly.

She sidled up to him, which surprised him and also made him nervous.

"You're doing *so* well, Gimlet! I'm so proud of you!"

"You——you are?" he stuttered. "I thought you never noticed me."

"I have! I certainly have."

She reached out a finger and gently touched his nose. Tiny hairs on the back of his neck stood on end.

"You're suddenly so smart and successful and ... *exceptional!*"

She leaned so close he could smell the scent of well-oiled cogs.

"We have so much in common," she whispered. "Me with my cogs and you with your sealant ..."

"My sealant?"

"We could go places, Gimlet! Together, we could run BOFFO!"

She leaned ever so close to him, closed her eyes and *CRASH!*

At the far end of the factory floor, Midge had dropped a case of glass toys at her feet. She stared at them for a second and then turned and ran from the room.

"I——I wonder if she heard us?" said Gimlet and suddenly, he felt the oddest sensation—as if someone was nibbling on his ear.

"*What's in the vats?*" whispered Ophelia.

"The vats?" Gimlet sighed. "The vats are ..."

He leapt back, suddenly frightened and angry.

"You want the secret of my toy!"

"No!" cried Ophelia. "It's just—you know—keeping secrets can be *so* lonely. Surely, you want to share them with—"

"No one!" said Gimlet, backing himself against a massive receptacle that made swishing and slogging sounds. "I'll never tell! *Never! The secret is mine!*"

Ophelia glared at him, her eyes ablaze.

"I was wrong about you, Gimlet! You *are* a scrawny little nothing! And that's all you ever will be!"

And with that, she spun around and stomped to the far edge of the factory floor. At the door, she turned to him one final time.

"*I can see you won't be needing any cogs!*" she said. And she slammed the door as she left.

Gimlet returned to his suite where he found Midge packing up all of her belongings.

"Midge?" he asked. "What are you doing?"

"Leaving," she said, trying her best to seem pleasant. "It's—it's just so *perfect* here, Gim. So many servants and machines and . . . there's nothing to improve! You know me. I've got to fix things or I'll go bonkers! I'm going to find somewhere—where someone needs me."

"But—but—*I need you*, Midge!" he pleaded.

"No, you don't," she said.

She picked up her bag and left. Gimlet stood there, dumbfounded, when all of a sudden, Rollo burst in, happy as a Maltese Shih Tzu and with a big package under his arm.

"Hel-lo!" said Rollo. "Where's Midge?"

"Gone," said Gimlet.

"Gone?" asked Rollo. "Gone where?"

"What's that?" asked Gimlet, staring at Rollo's bag.

"Oh, this? It's my *New Loaf!*" he exclaimed. And with great flair, he pulled out a loaf that looked quite a bit like his old *Hairy Loaf*, except this one was new, firm, sparklingly shiny, and slightly less hairy.

"And watch this!" said Rollo.

He took the *Loaf* and threw it as hard as he could at the ground. Amazingly, it bounced right back up and fell, gently as a feather, into his hands. Rollo grinned ear to ear, pleased with himself.

"How did it do that?" asked Gimlet.

"Well, it's unbreakable!" laughed Rollo. "I'm calling it—"

"*Who cares what you're calling it, Rollo?!*" barked Gimlet. "*How does it bounce?!*"

"Well, you know," said Rollo, "I—I—I—I—I—you know—I dropped it in our vat."

"*My* vat!" snarled Gimlet.

"Well—well—that is to say—" sputtered Rollo.

Gimlet's eyes widened and the tips of his ears seemed to suddenly get sharper. Rollo watched him, curiously. Gimlet grabbed the *Loaf* away from Rollo and growled at him, angrily.

"*Didn't you read the signs on the vats?!*" he cried. "*They were clearly marked!*"

"What? I—"

"Out! Get out of my suite! Get out of my factory! *Now!*"

"But—!"

"No buts! *Out!*"

And Gimlet ran around the suite, gathering up all of Rollo's belongings and tossing them at him, hatefully. He pushed Rollo toward the door.

"But—but Gimlet—you're my best friend!" said Rollo.

"*You're no friend of mine!*" said Gimlet, kicking Rollo out the door by the seat of the pants.

Rollo stared at Gimlet.

"Look at you," he said, flushly. "You're not the Gimlet I knew! You've become *mean! Hateful!* You've—you've become—*Sozgüd!* It's no wonder Midge left!"

And he walked out, just as Gimlet threw the *Loaf* after him. But the toy merely ricocheted off the door and smacked Gimlet back in the head.

Sozgüd? Had he become Sozgüd? Yes, it was true—he *had* been mean and proud and nasty. He didn't mean to be. He had just wanted to be *special! Important! For once in his life!* And now he was nothing but alone. *No Midge. No Rollo.* It was awful. What was the point of making an unbreakable toy if all you were left with was a terribly broken heart?

Things couldn't have gotten worse for Gimlet. But they got worse anyway. By the next morning, reports started coming in about all the horrible things people were doing with their *Gimlet* toys. Of course, they were all trying to break them. But in their efforts to break them they were causing massive destruction to everything else nearby. Children were destroying furniture. Babies were setting houses on fire. One construction worker leveled an entire apartment complex in a frivolous effort to damage his toy with dynamite. The more people bought *Gimlets*, the more obsessed they were with trying to wreck them. Now, it was late December and *Gimlets* had practically ruined the entire holiday.

The President of the United States called it *Gimlet Mania* and declared a National Emergency. He ordered armored troops to go directly to BOFFO to confiscate all of the factory machinery and vats and every *Gimlet* toy they could find, and to arrest any toy makers that appeared responsible.

By the time Gimlet heard the news, the GAT—along with Throttle and Clutch—had flown the coop. Meanwhile, all of the other toy makers were frantically packing up their belongings and riding off on their electric scooters in an effort to abandon BOFFO before anyone could mistake them for Gimlet.

Soon, the entire plant was deserted and Gimlet found himself not just completely alone but in imminent danger. He was terribly scared. Everything had turned rotten so quickly. He needed a plan. An idea.

A Brilliant Idea.

And then he realized he had one.

He ran to the kitchen cupboard, threw it open and began furiously searching the shelves. There, way in the back, he found one of Sozgüd's very first *Brilliant Idea!* packages. He tore it open and read the instructions.

They were simple instructions, written in a large, easy-to-read font. The instructions reminded Gimlet of how smart and good he surely was, and about how much true potential he likely definitely had. The instructions told Gimlet that really, he wasn't alone. That everyone everywhere was really *with him*, whether they knew it or not. And the instructions gave him permission to be his *absolute very best* and summon up that extra courage that he clearly had inside of him. Finally, Gimlet found the gold certificate decal inside the package and stuck it onto the upper left pocket of his shirt.

And in a very small but *real* way, he started to feel better.

And he actually did get an Idea, which was great timing, because at that moment eight dozen National Guard troops stormed into the plant knocking the main gates down with a deafening *KERWHOMP!*

Without hesitation, Gimlet threw clothes, his very first original *Gimlet* toy, and his *Brilliant Idea* package into a duffel bag and hopped out of his first-floor window into the chilly night air. He ran deep, deep into the nearby woods and didn't look back until he was far from the factory and too tired to travel anymore. Under a bushy, protective pine tree, he huddled up against his bag and tried to keep warm. And he thought of Midge and Rollo and how terrible he'd been to them and how much he wished they were with him now, so that he could apologize profusely to both of them. And, finally, he thought back to his new *Brilliant Idea,* the strength of which would keep him warm that night.

And the idea was this: that somehow or other—to set things right—he *must* find a way, once and for all, to break his unbreakable toy.

And with that, he fell fast asleep.

When he awoke the next morning, he was cozier and warmer than he had expected to be. But not because of warm ideas. No, it was because he was in a bed—a huge bed with blankets all wrapped round him.

"Well! Look who's up!" a voice called.

Gimlet couldn't believe his eyes. There, standing nearby, was Ida, Midge's long-lost mother. And bringing in a nice hot bowl of oatmeal was her long-lost father, Moe.

"*Ida! Moe!*" Gimlet cried, thrilled.

"Hello, Gimmie!" said Moe, setting down the oatmeal and settling into an old rocking chair. "Welcome to our new little hideaway in the woods! Gave us a mighty scare, lying down there out in the open, y'did!"

"But—but you were lost in that canyon refilling accident!" said Gimlet.

"Never was!" exclaimed Ida. "Job just took much much longer than either of us expected!"

"Y'should see it, now!" said Moe. "No more breathtakingly majestic hole in the ground of Adanac! Now, it's just perfect flat land—84 miles long!"

"But," said Ida, "we missed our little Midgie something awful."

"I bet," said Gimlet.

"We did discover one thing," said Moe. "We are *sick of perfection!*"

"Oh, yes," said Ida. "Seems like the world's been trying all too hard to be perfect—or *somebody's* idea of perfect! Seems to us what it really needs is to be just a wee bit messier!"

"So, now we're committed to helping people mess things up, good and awful!" said Moe. "That's our new philosophy!"

"I'm awfully glad you're home," said Gimlet.

"Me, too," said a familiar voice.

Gimlet turned and there, at the door, were Midge and Rollo.

"Midge! Rollo!" cried Gimlet and he leapt up and hugged both of them. "Can you ever forgive me? I was such a Sozgüd!"

"Yes, you were," agreed Midge.

"Now, tell us," said Moe, "what were you doing out there in the cold?"

And so, Gimlet told the four of them everything; about his original toy falling into the bucket, and how no other bucket of sealant acted the way that that first one did.

"Hold on," interrupted Rollo. "This cleaning bucket—was it outside Maintenance Room 14B?"

"I think so," said Gimlet.

"Well," continued Rollo, "I had a big accident in Room 14B earlier that morning. I was in there looking for something to trim the hairs on my loaf—when I suddenly heard Sozgüd out in the hallway. Well, I panicked and accidentally knocked a jar of liquid Plooze into a maintenance bucket which I thought was empty at the time. But it must have had sealant in it! At that point, I was so late for the New Toy Day presentation that I ran out of Room 14B and forgot all about it!"

"The Plooze in the sealant," started Midge.

"Must've created a *super*-sealant!" added Ida.

"An *unbreakable* sealant!" continued Moe.

"But if it is a super-sealant," said Gimlet, "how could we ever un-seal it?"

"You leave that to us," said Ida, with a bright gleam in her eye. "I'll bet we can mess it up good."

All through the night, the five labored to de-assemble, mis-fabricate, and un-build the component parts of Gimlet's super-sealant. Finally, at 4:32 a.m., exhausted and sleepless, they stared at their creation: a *Mega Super-UnSealing Liquid*.

They went outside and Gimlet placed his original *Gimlet* toy smack dab in the middle of the road. Slowly, he poured the entire contents of the bucket over it, while the others watched, anxiously. The new clear liquid soaked the toy and then evaporated onto the ground.

Gimlet knelt down, picked up the toy and gingerly brought it to Midge.

"You do the honors," he said.

Midge lifted the toy high over her head and flung it to the ground with all of her might. And Gimlet's *Unbreakable Gimlet* shattered into a million, million pieces.

And that's pretty much the end of the story.

Except for this last little part.

The next day—Christmas Day—Gimlet, Midge, and Rollo all went on live national TV with the President of the United States and, before millions of captivated viewers, they broke an *Unbreakable Gimlet*. And they promised free bottles of their *Magical Gimlet Breaking Liquid* to anyone who requested it. No shipping or handling charges required. Later, they discovered that their brief demonstration had the highest TV ratings of the entire past century.

In January, the three friends moved back into Bungalow 37 which was still deserted because all of the owners and toy makers had abandoned BOFFO for glorious new careers at the other leviathan toy companies in Bandersnatch Valley, Utah—especially *Flurflang*—where they all did reasonably well.

Midge was excited because their abandoned toy factory had so much dust and decay that she likely had decades of improvements to look forward to. Despite her parents' change of philosophy, Midge remained very much a Perfectionist.

And they decided to have one last *Brilliant Idea*. They realized that they now had an entire manufacturing plant with machines and robots, but they were quite sick of making toys. So, they converted the plant into the world's biggest and best-ever bakery.

And their specialty was a tremendously tasty—and just *slightly* hairy—

Loaf.

Bits & Pieces

GOOD EVENING. THANKS FOR COMING. WHAT A GREAT-looking crowd. Alright. Let's all settle down. Before we begin weighing in on the relative discursiveness of Kierkegaard in relation to Hobbes's critique of the Diaspora, I'd just like to say that there is too much fucking snow. Yes, I'm sorry, but there's just too much fucking snow. And I wrote this joke a month ago. In the middle of January. And back then there was too much fucking snow and now there is really way too much fucking snow. It's like Hoth out there. I mean—it's surreal. How long has this been going on now? Weeks? Months? Jesus. I feel like I've got a perpetual snow hangover. I shoveled for three hours this morning. *Again*. And then my mother called from Florida. *Why don't you get a snowblower?!* Uhm . . . why don't you go fuck yourself? Love you! Sorry. I didn't say that. I didn't say "love you."

You know it's cold when you're watching Mideast riot coverage and thinking—wow, looks cozy. *Honey—what are we doing for Spring Break? How 'bout Syria?*

So, a month ago, when I was preparing for tonight, there was too much fucking snow. And now—*now*—there is still really way *way* too much fucking snow.

Actually, a month ago, I thought, well, what if it isn't still true in a month? What if I prepare this and rehearse it over and over and then a a a a a a a freaking meteor hits New Jersey opening up an active volcano that spews hot magma everywhere—and it all just melts? That might change things. But no, no—here we are. Here we are. And I'll bet you fifty dollars—right now—that a month from now, there will still be too much fucking snow.

I've got my love to keep me warm. But an electric blanket would be nice. Or a space heater.

I just bought a snowplow. It's an old-fashioned snowplow. Now, I just need four horses to pull it.

You know who I feel sorry for? My dog. Especially in negative thirty-degree weather. I can't imagine having to go outside every time you have to pee. I couldn't do it. *I'm just going to use this corner of the room, today. Don't mind me! I'm just—I'm gonna go behind the couch. I'll go outside tomorrow for sure. Look—I'll just—I'll cover it up with this T-shirt. You'll never know it's there.*

Actual reminder on all Fed Ex shipping materials: PLEASE DO NOT SHIP LIQUIDS, BLOOD OR FLUIDS IN THIS PACKAGING. Well, there go all my Christmas gifts.

There are a lot of things I hate in life: poverty, cruelty to animals. But nothing so much as Styrofoam packing chips. I *hate* Styrofoam packing chips. The kind that are 50 percent Styrofoam, 50 percent static cling. They don't biodegrade. They have a half-life of two million years. I used to like getting packages. Now, it's like being in a Stephen King novel. You don't even want to open the box. But it's

Christmas—and you open it, and suddenly these things are swarming all over you like Styrofoam insects. *And they're clinging, clinging—and flying everywhere into the air— and they're creeping up your hands and your throat and choking you! And you're wrapping plastic bags around your hands trying to get them into the garbage!* And finally, you get through all of the Styrofoam packing chips and get to the bottom of the box just to discover the imitation pewter ice bucket that you never wanted. So, please, just send a card. Or call. But please don't send anything in Styrofoam packing chips.

I just got the latest holiday drink at Starbucks, the *Dean Martin Roast.* It went down sloppy, but smooth.

My mom is the sweetest person I know. Every year, for my birthday, my mom sends me a cake in the mail from Cincinnati to New Jersey. But she doesn't send it UPS, or have it delivered from a local bakery. No, what she does is she buys a cake—and stuffs it in a box surrounded by Styrofoam packing chips—and then mails it to me fourth class, because it's cheaper. So, three or four weeks after my birthday I get a big box in the mail and inside will be a giant mound of brown sludge shoved up against the side—and it will say something like—"Hap- Blldgzshgdlgl." I'm always impressed that she doesn't light the candles first before sending it. So, I get this gift a month late—no card—I don't know what it is because somehow, I forget, year after year. I'll come home to the FBI and a pack of dogs circling around this package. *Mr. Bernstein, this could be the work of terrorists.* No, no, I say, it's just my mother. She loves me. So yes, getting this cake is always a little weird and creepy and crazy. *But I eat it!* Of course, I eat it. I mean, I'm not gonna waste a perfectly good mound of stale, cakey chocolate sludge.

It always warms my heart to see the giant Hanukkah Bush at Rockefeller Center.

Y'know what always said Christmas to me? That old commercial of Santa riding the giant Norelco electric shaver down the snowy mountain. Wasn't that the best?

Christmas is coming! Christmas is coming! Santa's on the shaver! Don't ride on the wrong side, Santa! Finally, when I was older, someone actually gave me a Norelco electric shaver—and wow, it really sucked. Not a close shave. And I guess the tip-off should've been Santa's long white beard, right? I mean—*clearly not a user.* And then I didn't know what to do. Re-gift it or take it outside and jump on it like a toboggan. *Whee!* But how stupid would that have been?

'Tis better to re-gift than re-receive.

I love all of the holidays. My wife was raised Italian Catholic. So, basically, I married her so I could do Christmas. So, we're an interfaith couple. And my parents were interfaith, and my grandparents were interfaith. So, I come from a long line of religious ambivalence. My wife and I had an interfaith wedding. We had a priest *and* a rabbi perform the ceremony. And we threw in two judges and a monkey just for good measure. It was actually very difficult finding a rabbi who would perform the ceremony in a church. I finally found the most reformed rabbi I'd ever met on Craig's List. He was tremendously accommodating. For two grand he'd not only perform the service, but he'd do it juggling fire sticks on a unicycle. So, that was a pretty good deal and only a few of the missalettes caught fire.

By the way, it's a real commitment being interfaith. Finding that fence, parking yourself on top of it and defending your goddamn right to stay there in the middle. There's tons of pressure to pick sides. But, to this day, we remain fanatically indecisive.

I vividly remember the first time I went to my in-laws for Christmas, because it was like Disney On Ice for me. We got there and everything was beautiful and perfect. There was twenty feet of snow. And inside there was a huge tree with Waterford Crystal ornaments and stockings over the mantelpiece. I was so excited! I was like—*let's make egg-nog snowmen! Or whatever it is you do! Where's the figgy pudding?! That's a thing, right? Let's wassail! Whatever wassailing is—I want to wassail! I want to wassail right now!* And they're looking at me, like *what the hell is wrong with you?* Because they don't really think about it that way anymore. I mean, they love the holiday, sure—but now they're too busy arguing about *do we need 32 trays of cookies for four people or should we make 38*?

I got my dog the cutest little holiday sweater and he looks great. But now all the other dogs in the neighborhood tease him. *Hey Ace! Who dressed you today?! Your Master? Ruff ruff ruff!* Dog jerks.

I love Hanukkah, too, by the way. I'd like to love it even more. But every year something about the holiday makes me crazy. First off, no one really knows what it's about. *What's it about?* See, you don't know. I'll tell you the true meaning of Chanukah: it's the closest Jewish holiday we have to Christmas. That's it. Whichever holiday we have that's closest to Christmas—bad weather for goats, wearing three-cornered hats—that's the one where we're giving gifts. *Hey, kids! Bring in the goats! Put on your three-cornered hats! It's time to give gifts! And here's some hats for the goats.*

So, anyway, we don't know what Hanukkah is about and we don't know *when* it is. Because Jews have a fluid calendar! This year, Hanukkah is three weeks early. Next year, it's in June. Let me ask my Jewish friends this: How did you find out when Chanukah is this year? One of your top five major holidays? *Google.* You googled it. Non-Jews:

How many of you googled *When is Christmas?* Exactly. Can you even conceive of *not knowing* when Christmas is? Of course not. Because early Christians were geniuses. They didn't just fix the date, they made everyone else on the planet switch to their calendar. That's a Brilliant Idea.

I actually have friends that go: *When was Hanukkah? Last Tuesday? Aw, crap! Missed it again. Sorry kids! Maybe next year!*

We can't even agree on how to *spell* the holiday. Is it *Chhhhanukah?* Or is it *Hanukkkkkah?* We don't know. I see Facebook chats where people go: *How's your Chanukah going? Great, how's your Hanukkah going? I dunno. I forgot to check Google. I think it was last week.*

What bothers me most about Hanukkah though is— in corporate America—they bring out this enormous spectacular Christmas tree covered with fantastic ornaments and baubles—and they bring it out before Halloween. But then for Hanukkah—they bring out this tiny, crappy, electric menorah. It's not even a cool, modern one. It's a broken one from the 1970s with bulbs that used to be night lights. So, Hanukkah has gone from the *Festival of Lights* to the *Twisting of the Bulbs.* Hey kids—*who wants to twist a bulb?! Twist the shamash first, honey! Start on the left!*

And then, the day after Hanukkah at work—*BAM!*— menorah goes back in the closet. I asked the HR guy at my company *why don't you leave it out a few days? It's so nice and festive with its shitty little bulbs. Let's all enjoy it for a few more days.* And he goes, *no, no, holiday's over. It would be inappropriate.* What's inappropriate? You know he's not running around the Monday after Christmas going—*get the tree down! What if someone sees?*

Then he actually said to me, *well, we don't want to leave the menorah on because it eats up too much power.* He actually said that. *Really? Is it gonna blow a fuse? New York blackout caused by shitty little menorah. Film at 11.*

And now, New Year's Eve is just around the corner and half a block from the liquor store.

I was buying gifts for the holidays. My son wanted a car, but my son's a terrible driver. So, I bought him a Driver's-Ed car. The kind that has brakes on both the driver's side and the passenger side. So, now when I'm with him, I go *too fast!* and slam on the brakes.

He wanted a Nintendo Switch. He already has an XBOX and a PSP and a Nintendo 3DS. I just get confused. We never had any of that stuff when I was a kid. We had a SWPPT—a slightly warped ping-pong table. Later we upgraded to a SWPPT-BN—a slightly warped ping-pong table with a broken net. And later my parents had it reconfigured into a SWPPT-BN-PCPTMO—a slightly warped ping-pong table with a broken net that people could put their margaritas on.

My all-time favorite Chanukah gift when I was a kid was a *G.I. Joe with Real Facial Hair!* He was incredibly cool and he came with an axe and camping gear. But I don't think it was real facial hair. It was more like real Velcro facial hair. If they sold it today, it would probably be *G.I. Joe with Hipster Douche Beard!* and instead of an axe he'd probably come with oversized Bose headphones and a can of LaCroix.

I had a pretty good week off during the holidays.

I did a lot of adult things and was very manly: I built things and fixed things and drank beer and lived in my man cave. And now I'm completely out of testosterone.

I tried Zumba but was disappointed to learn that simply saying *Zumba!* did not turn me into Captain Marvel.

I stared into the abyss, but the abyss was too busy watching *Tiger King*.

I went on a carb-free diet and then a crab-free diet. So, I gave up croutons and crustaceans.

I achieved inner peace for about thirteen seconds and then I had to shovel snow again. And there is still really way, way, way too much fucking snow.

Last year, around this time, three Santa Clauses—two tall ones and a short, fat, jolly one—followed me down onto the subway. I didn't think they were following *me*, per se. But still, there they were. It was rush hour and the subway car was packed. Not sardines packed, but full. And I pressed myself up against the back wall, which is where I stand when I'm standing in a crowded subway car. And the Santas were nearby, huddled together. One of the tall ones had his iPhone turned up way too loud. The other ate a sandwich from a bag.

And after a minute I noticed that all three seemed to be staring at me and nodding and whispering. And I thought, *nah, they're not looking at me.* But they were. And then everyone in the car was staring at them staring at me, some smirking. And I was creeped out and pissed. Then one of the Santas—the short, fat jolly one—lifted his hand and pointed a finger at my crotch.

I looked down—and saw that my fly was open.

So, I turned to the back wall, nonchalantly, and zipped up. When I turned back, the short Santa nodded and smiled: *good job.* The iPhone Santa gave me a thumbs up.

And I said the only thing you really could say at that point:

Merry Christmas!

So—

Happy Whatever the Hell you Celebrate! And don't forget to leave some cookies out.

Reading Group Guide

For the purposes of group discussion, we present the following questions to help enrich and invigorate your reading.

1. OMG, what was *that* all about?
2. Why were there no orchids on the cover?
3. For that matter, why were there no orchids in the book?
4. Conjugate the entire novel.
5. Discuss the refreshing absence of *Magic Realism*.
6. Discuss the incessant use of the phrase "beer-goggles."
7. Discuss my hat at length.
8. No, c'mon—keep going.
9. Does anyone have any Kleenex?
10. At what point did you fall asleep and why?
11. Who brought the babka? Wow, that was good, wasn't it? I can never make anything that good at

my house! You bought it? *You didn't!* Really? Where?!

12. When Twyla says Gordo is "full of vinegar"— what the hell is she talking about? I mean, full of vinegar? Literally? Full of vinegar? He's full of vinegar?

13. Next time, can we please pick something with a few more chicks in it?

14. Screw men! *HA HA HA HA HA!* Oh, oh—not you, Bill. Sorry! Damn, you look good tonight. Wait—did I say that out loud?

15. What was the significance of the—of—of—oh, forget it.

16. What was the question, again?

17. Book club? *Oh shit! I thought this was Bunco.*

About the Author

Alex Bernstein is the award-winning author of *Miserable Adventure Stories* and *Plrknib*. His work has appeared at *McSweeney's*, *NewPopLit*, *The Big Jewel*, *The American Bystander*, *Gi60*, *Yankee Pot Roast*, *Swink*, *Litro*, *Back Hair Advocate*, *Corvus*, *BluePrintReview*, *Hobo Pancakes*, *The Rumpus*, *The Legendary*, *MonkeyBicycle*, and *PopImage*, among numerous others. Please visit him at www.promonmars.com. His most recent book, *Miserable Love Stories*, published in February 2020.